Market Books
85 Cameron Street
Whangarei N.Z.

Blood

Geoff Cochrane

Victoria University Press

VICTORIA UNIVERSITY PRESS
Victoria University of Wellington
PO Box 600 Wellington

© Geoff Cochrane 1997

ISBN 0 86473 326 7

First published 1997

This book is copyright. Apart from
any fair dealing for the purpose of private study,
research, criticism or review, as permitted under the
Copyright Act, no part may be reproduced by any
process without the permission of
the publishers

Published with the assistance of a grant from

Printed by Wright and Carman (NZ) Ltd, Wellington

For Lindsay Rabbitt

'The natural flight of the human mind is not from pleasure to pleasure but from hope to hope.'

Samuel Johnson

One

The light above the hills was a flourish, a watery stripe gone wrong. He climbed toward the convent. A door had been left open for Abel. The varnished floor creaked. A little way along the corridor, the cassocks and surplices hung on hooks. The cassocks were red. When Abel had dressed he passed the room where the priest had spent the night. In the light from a bare bulb, the priest stood reading his breviary. His soutane gave him the appearance of having a long back and a slender waist. How odd it was for a priest to have hair like that, so wavy and blond. Was he vain, the priest, for having hair like that?

Abel was too much aware of possibilities.

Mother Clementine had a face dark and ancient. She had lived in Japan and *that* might change your skin. Perhaps she was really an Indian, a squaw. Abel met her in a room full of plants, vases of burnished brass and ceramic pots. The place resembled a glasshouse. He would live in it if he could, though he was a boy. It was full of rich and complementary scents, of unburned incense and flowers and candle wax. And Mother Clementine had her smells, those of the laundry and garden, of yellow soap and soil. She was wistful and gentle, unlike other nuns. The silver rims of her spectacles seemed to match the slight sibilance of her speech.

'The O'Brien boy was coming, but his mother is terribly ill. They had the doctor to her in the night. You must remember her in your prayers, Abel.'

The mass took place in a chapel of white marble. Abel could hear the girls of the convent behind him, saying their responses or turning the pages of their missals in unison. They sang parts of the liturgy with a ringing sweetness. Could voices be white? They seemed so to Abel. Soon he must take the cruets of wine and water to the priest. Then came the consecration, that radiant core at the centre of the engine, the heart of the machine of ritual.

It had the purity of an equation, the gaunt persuasiveness of a basic sum. Here was the bread and here the yellow wine; that their transubstantiation should be invisible did not much deflate the miracle. And when the priest elevated the Host, it was Abel's job to tap a golden bell with a mallet swathed in velvet. The chime was like an odour. It passed out from the altar in a single vibrant pulse, shimmering and full. A tone contained by the walls of the chapel made Abel's skull vibrate like a tine. The arm with which he had caused the sound felt responsible and good.

There might be bacon and eggs when he got home. The warm reek of bedding and urine would come from the room he shared with his brother. Abel's was the top bunk. To the wall above it he had fixed a shelf. On this stood a Mitchell bomber he had built from a plastic kit. He had painted it brown and green, the insect colours of camouflage. The domes of its machine-gun turrets shone with a toy translucency. Beside it were stored his modeller's paints, his fishing-reel and chess set. On the wall above his pillow was a wooden crucifix. The Jesus pinned to it was made of a tinny alloy. Behind the crucifix was tucked a Palm Sunday sprig, now desiccated and bleached by sunlight.

Jerry Vale was on the radio.

'I told you to polish your shoes,' Aunt Ellen said. 'It's too late now to be doing them.' She took a plate from the oven. 'See what you can do with your brother. He's wet the bed again and won't get up.'

Conrad was lying dead beneath his bedding. He would never acknowledge shame about his wetting. Instead he cultivated the abandonment of limbs.

'There's nice fried bread,' said Abel.

'Nuh,' Conrad muttered.

'What's *nuh* supposed to mean?'

'Just leave him if he's going to be silly.'

'Nuh, nuh, nuh,' chanted Conrad, the sounds upholstered by blankets.

Abel's breakfast was on the table. He sat down to it. Aunt Ellen scratched his scalp through his hair. Her lower lip was wet and her breath smelled of tea. Abel would save the yolk of his egg till last. But when he got to school the monitor would mark him for dirty shoes.

Two

I know nothing of my own life. It's opaque to me; I've forgotten it.

My name is Abel Blood. I'm not quite old enough to have served in Vietnam, yet I suffer all the psychoses of that war, that invasion, all the tics and traumas that scar the invader's psyche. And in my youth I made an experiment of my own in living, in behaviour.

Who would be a writer? Better to dig for coal; better to sell one's blood for the next fix. The decision to write is formed of an acrid pall, the smoke from the ruins of manlier aspirations. I really want to refuse to eat or work, to deny the world my slightest collaboration, to let the years expend themselves while I swig my life away in some dim bar.

Yet, and yet –

She was a nice aunt. The poverty of our household was unfair to her. She'd been a gracious hostess, a generous giver of parties, but now her petticoat hung in a visible band beneath the hem of her dress. She deserved smarter clothes. There were things she didn't know and couldn't feel. We were ashamed of her, a little bit ashamed. It seems to me that Conrad and I didn't much champion her. We weren't allowed to call her Mother, Mum, but with what a glow of earnest and impotent longing we wanted to do just that.

Conrad's memory of his mother was fresher than mine. People die. They are killed every day, suffocated by phlegm or blasted forward through windshields. Our parents had died in the sea in perfect weather. He had drowned attempting to rescue her from a rip, that was the received wisdom. My brother would miss his mother from time to time, waking to lie disconsolate in the dark. His sorrow was deeply rational and loyal. Aunt Ellen would come and take his head in her arms. I could remember the smell of my mother's knees, an odour of nylon stockings and sun-warmed flesh. We were together on a lawn in sunshine. A young man was present, more upright than my mother. His shoes were black and his trousers grey and wide. He remains a summer ghost. I have never been able to win for him any more permanence or clarity than that he shares with the moon in daylight. There attaches to his niggling, specious image, or is bred of it or breathed out of it, the odour of that veneer of leathery stuff on his Kodak camera.

The pictures he took on the lawn have come down to me, glossy prints of good quality. My father is not in any. In the snaps he took of Conrad and my mother, she appears as a pretty, auburn type, a plump-armed woman of the early Fifties, generic and representative. My father seems to have gone for sturdy compositions. And put the sun behind him.

Aunt Ellen was our mother's widowed sister. She stood in a skewed relation to her community. Impediments and birthmarks were of interest to her. Her memory stocked and guaranteed all the most pungent information about people, but what she knew she feared and couldn't relish. She was vigilant and wrong, always in error despite her watchfulness. Nothing ever became wholly familiar to her. For instance, the neighbours' cars made her nervous: she could identify none of them. And she dreaded the spies and crooks night would send, dispatch to our very door. Thus developed her habit of inserting knives in the door jamb to impede forced entry. As the years passed she used more and more knives, the entire contents of the cutlery drawer sometimes. No one came. But I had seen her madness, barbarous runes beneath a mantle of leaves. Inside her wept and bled some memory of disaster, a wound inflicted early, never to be healed by merely adult endeavour. In order to be

11

Three

Aunt Ellen had an unmarried brother. He was, of course, an uncle to Conrad and me. When I was in my early teens, he came to live with us. Perhaps Athol Lye was slightly daft. The epileptic seizures of his childhood had disrupted his schooling. His hair was perfectly white and fine and he had it barbered often. When he shaved he used a Colgate stick of soap and a razor he assembled from its component parts. His chin was cleft into two blue hemispheres; these he lathered and shaved until they shone. He would have liked our modern aftershaves, the aesthetic of men's toiletries. A gentlemen's club employed him as a cleaner. His wardrobe was extensive and tasteful, marked by his liking for shoes in shades of brown. What he earned he spent, a circumstance that sometimes caused his sister irritation.

Uncle Athol was an energetic Catholic who wore a scapula, carried a rosary and kept an altar in his room. This garish personal shrine was even then a source of embarrassment to me. He was uxorious in the maintenance of this tinselled exhibit, carrying flowers to the plaster image of the Virgin Mary, seldom to Aunt Ellen.

'That's a good picture at the Tudor,' says Athol.

'You've seen it already?' I ask.

'He accidentally photographs a corpse in a park.'

We sit in an amber dusk. I'm thinking here of a warm afternoon, the room's waxy blinds rolled up and the front door open. Somewhere a fly is trapped and will succumb. At one end of the dining-room table, Athol has spread his paints and oil and turps. He wears spectacles in order to be drawn closer to the numbered shapes on the canvas board before him. He paints with slowness but no discernible skill.

'Should we have that bit of ham for tea?' asks Ellen.

'He drives a sports car and has his hair long,' says Athol. He is savouring the film he has seen.

'It's got a certificate,' I say.

'You won't be going to that then,' says Ellen.

'It wouldn't do him any harm,' says Athol.

'*You* wouldn't think so, no,' Ellen says. 'And I've told you to mind that table. I'm always on at you to put more paper down.'

'I have. Three sheets.'

'The turps is getting through, can't you see? I can't keep a thing. You were the same when we were children.'

'You should learn to forget things.'

'I was given a beautiful doll, don't you remember? It had lovely china eyes that opened and shut. And you and Ginger Russell smashed it up, broke it against the tree where we had the swing.'

'We never.'

'All my lovely things spoiled or broken. They couldn't give you a hiding because you had fits.'

'I wish they *had* thrashed me.'

'My plaits were the longest in the neighbourhood. You used to swing on them until I screamed.'

Athol has had enough. He puts his brush in a jar of turpentine and begins to fit the caps to his little wells of paint. 'There's no peace in this house,' he says.

'No? You couldn't bully me with John around. Even as a boy he was a gentleman. He knew how to make his way in the world.'

'He knew how to stay out of uniform, you mean. And who got all his thousands when he died, if he thought so much of you?'

'I could have done with a bit, it's true, what with Abel and

13

little Connie.'

I offer Athol a Stuyvesant cigarette. He takes it though he seldom smokes. His Spanish scene is full of sunny ochres, but the man emerging from the vine-covered arch goes vacant and unpainted.

Beginning when he saw

Four

Father Pears was moving slowly from desk to desk. 'Awake, Blood?'

Conrad said he was.

'At what stage of the development of the human foetus does the soul enter it?'

'At no stage, Father,' said Conrad.

'Does it not have one, boy?'

'Yes, Father.'

'Explain yourself.'

'It's there from the beginning.'

'It's there from the beginning? Why is it unlikely, Shaw, that the Church will approve the use by Catholics of the contraceptive pill?'

'Don't know, Father.'

'These are questions you'll face in the fifth form, if your teachers are enterprising. The Pope and the College of Cardinals are waiting to hear if the effect of the pill is to prevent conception or to destroy an established zygote. You follow?'

'Not really,' said Shaw.

'You, Neale. In the case of a zygote being flushed from the wall of the uterus by the action of a pill, what might be said to be taking place?'

'Abortion, Father?'

'You think so? Your answer will not prevent your most vigorous flagellation if you don't learn to sit erectly, however. How should you sit?'

'Erectly.'

'You find this word amusing, Fitzgerald? And what have you done to your book? Had your breakfast off it, eh? I am your science master, but we are entering an age when the light of clear moral thinking will increasingly need to be shone on ostensibly physical questions. Is there any boy whose father had trouble elucidating the concept of an isotope? This is a splendid drawing, Slain. I wish more boys would rid themselves of the notion that good draughtsmanship is effeminate.' The priest looked at his watch. 'Have I ever told you about the engineer I met in Bogotá?'

'No, Father,' Finch lied gamely.

The priest hitched his soutane, sat down on an empty desk and rested his feet on a chair. All the boys relaxed. Father Pears liked warmth. Before the class began, Finch had ensured that the gas heater was glowing pinkly. This was the first period of the afternoon. There were only Art and English ahead; the rest of the day would unfold itself sedately. Conrad glanced out at the empty playground. The sky to the north and west showed stark gaps of blue. Its stains of wetness dwindling in the wind, the asphalt of the yard was drying rapidly. The mesh of a fence somewhere clinked and clashed; the air could be heard swooping through it in gusts. Conrad and his classmates had listened before to the story about the Scottish engineer who drank absinth. Absinth made the heart grow fonder. The engineer would talk in a curtained bar about the displacement of water, and when his money ran out he would try to sell his special draughting pens, pens for every purpose in a kid-covered box. The water was in the story to make it instructive.

There was a knock at the door at the back of the room. The rector entered. All the boys stood up but the rector waved them down. He was an older man than Father Pears. He wore a clerical suit and his face was fleshy and brown, yet Conrad thought he had the ancient ugliness of a pioneer, a man in a photograph, stiff-necked and puritanical, made by the camera to seem wall-eyed, perhaps even blind. His mood was often whimsical and kind; today, however, he seemed somewhat constrained, a little glum and childish.

'If I may, Father Pears,' he said, now standing at the front of the class. 'Boys will note that the wind is dropping. Power will soon be restored to the college. It's worth remembering that when electricity fails, all appliances should be turned off at the wall. You'll find this tip invaluable in the home and workplace. You have a home, Rhys-Smith?'

'Yes, Father.'

'I'm pleased to hear it. Let us hope it has not been burned down in your absence. We must not have mendicant boys cluttering the streets. Where are you, Blood? Ah. Would you be so kind, with Father Pears' permission, to come with me to my study? Thank you, Father.'

Again the boys stood. Conrad felt a hand on his shoulder, guiding him from the classroom. The air outside the prefab was fresh. Now the sun was out, it made the windows of the science block white and opaque, made a sunny aisle along the building, a cloister Conrad must walk with the rector. Soon they entered a covered way and were in gloom for a moment; when they emerged the back of the old college was at hand, a grey place to which Conrad aspired, wanted with a spiritual fervour to have more frequent cause to enter. The rector removed his hand from the boy's shoulder. In. The lovely place was silent at this hour, the stairs seeming broad and the landings spacious. The priest and Conrad climbed. And the light on the landings was captive and still, interior and clean, like that in a Dutch painting. There were places of dimness, too, from which stood out the brass of the fingerplates and handles of doors, like things in a museum.

'It certainly blew,' said the rector. He was speaking of the mystery of spring, in which there is something of autumn, Conrad thought, of tawny pollens and dusts, airborne, migratory.

'Why do you want to see me, Father?'

'I have . . . There is need . . . Abel will be present.' The priest had skin the colour of tobacco; his hands and face were as dark as the sailor's. He opened the door to his study and there was light, the plain light of the city, of a cirrus-streaked sky. 'When I die, which will not be long, God will have many things to forgive me, little brother. This is my cat, which forgives me everything.'

The cat was standing just inside the door, its tail tremulous. It was young and black with white mask and socks. It made an intelligent mew of greeting, its mouth a wedge of pink gristle, its teeth like cilia. The rector went to the window and raised it to its fullest extent; it seemed to jam with a squeak. Thin smears of cloud dusted the sky in places. Below, at a level with the window, the tops of trees were visible, their leaves wet with light, and Conrad could hear a bird, the plump, sucking cheep and chup of a sparrow.

This was the sound of sorrow. Or the sob of boldest joy.

'There are stranger things than death,' said the rector. He was seated now at his desk beneath a painting of a former incumbent of his office. 'This wait is irksome. Would you like my job, Blood? Have you ever thought of becoming a priest?'

'I've thought of being a monk,' Conrad said. 'I don't think I'd like it much.'

Abel knocked and entered the study quietly: he had found the door ajar.

'At last,' said the rector. 'There should be another chair – I've spoken to the caretaker about bringing one up. You'll have to rest at your oars, so to speak. Come closer, Conrad. You'll both have to meet what I have to say with a measure of courage and optimism. This morning a policeman was called to your house by a neighbour. A doctor has examined your Aunt Ellen and found her to be ill. It seems her mind is affected.'

Abel glanced at Conrad before he spoke. 'She broke a lot of crockery last night. What will happen to her?'

'She'll not be there when you get home, alas. Your aunt has been taken to a hospital skilled in dealing with cases of dementia. There she'll be assessed and suitable treatment started. We must pray that soon her state of mind will permit her to be returned to you.'

Five

I capitulated. I gave way to convenience, to the promise of no longer having to share her suffering. Her misery had become a shocking spectacle. We connived with exterior forces to have her removed from her home. Let the asylum have her – she'd become unbearable.

Frightened and tentative, Athol rang the hospital that night. He was asked not to come.

The evening wore on like an undeserved holiday, a shameful truancy. I made Welsh rabbit for the three of us, discovering how filthy the stove had become, how stale and sparse the contents of the safe. Conrad was in awe of the situation. Athol wept as he did the dishes.

The following Saturday, we went to Porirua. My memory assembles the impression of a train ride, a brief condition of boredom. We met Aunt Ellen in what I think was a sun porch. Already the system was doing its work. I watched the chloral hydrate brought round like cordial. Though Ellen mistook Conrad for me and me for my dead father, a rancorous hatred of her own condition coexisted with her confusion. I had read that dementia like hers was characterised by spells of lucidity, that during these the sufferer experienced an overwhelming anxiety or grief, you could take your pick. Don't ask me what was said. Don't ask me to reinvent and order the attempts Aunt Ellen made to scale the wall between us. She was glad we had come; she would get her things. Better late than never; the nurse would ring a taxi; poor Mrs Clark would be sorry to see her go. Her knees and lap seemed much reduced, enfeebled. She was wearing a gingham dress, a pattern she would never have worn in life, in her own home or about her neighbourhood.

Through a window I could see the interior of the ward from which she had been brought. Above the lolling heads of the patients, a television screen delivered soundless bursts of light. It was silent, had been silenced. I grasped the idea that Ellen was meant to die in this place, fade and diminish and die. She had been made as unattractive as a moulting bird in a cage. The question our experiment asked was this: if you break a heart, how soon will the body follow it into extinction? I was indignant. Had the means presented itself, I would have murdered her.

Over days and weeks and months she endured. For years she persisted. She became gaunt and tiny, a stubborn scrap of life, an infamy and an accusation always at the edge of my thoughts. How bitterly accusatory and damning was her continued existence, however insubstantial. She shamed and damned us all, becoming slightly deaf, though never so deaf that she was not alert to Mrs Clark's every faltering movement. She'd found a friend in Bedlam and I'd stopped visiting her.

I was in the sixth form when Ellen was committed. One day I got to the gate of the college but couldn't enter the grounds. In an elemental corner of the Botanic Garden, I began to read the letters of DH Lawrence.

People came to the house in Lyall Bay, a man and a woman like meter-readers, like the agents of a basic utility, with papers in a briefcase. They found Athol gruesomely engaging: he showed them his altar and most-recent paintings. Conrad should go to a foster home. The arrangements were made and he went off, departed in a taxi with the new people. They seemed timid and good and likely to be hurt. And Conrad kept returning to our sandy floorboards, to the chops and tomatoes Athol and I had for tea.

Having only the faintest odour of

Six

Abel Blood and Lincoln Dorne were walking along an esplanade at night. They had been to a screening of Jean Cocteau's *Orphée* at a house on a hill behind them. 'How did they get effects like that?' asked Lincoln.

'They printed the negative backward frame by frame.'

The bones behind Abel's ears were so cold they hurt. The sea beyond the wall to his right could not be seen in the blackness. Abel and his friend were silent for a while.

'They'd have to act backwards,' Lincoln said.

'It gave their faces an odd plasticity.'

'Good, though, the whole thing. The bikies in black, the poet in the car getting messages on the radio.'

The esplanade was still, the cars all parked and locked. An icy radiance came off the sea. Pink puddles crawled with tiny ripples. Abel was glad he had gone to the film. He felt newly mobile and adroit. A secret had been imparted to him. Night was his medium. He dipped along like a limousine, superior and fluid. If this was a result of the dope he had smoked, the movie's pagan liturgy had awed him.

No surf could be heard. Down from the blackest sky snow began to crowd, unhindered and fleet. It seemed to exercise consciousness and skill in the way it fell.

'I've never been in this before,' said Lincoln. 'It just seems to materialise.'

Flakes poured through the windless air. And the young men walked through them.

'There's a chick up ahead,' said Abel. 'What's she doing out?'

Lincoln said nothing. A young woman stood with her back to the sea. She was looking toward Abel and Lincoln. Abel thought the snow might be falling with more hurry where she was standing. As he and Lincoln were about to pass her, she spoke.

'There's a man in my kitchen.'

Lincoln halted promptly, Abel with some reluctance.

'And shouldn't he be?' asked Lincoln.

'He wasn't there when I went to bed. I think he's eating Weet-Bix.'

'It's an outrage,' said Lincoln to Abel.

'If you two are too windy . . .'

'Which house is it?' asked Abel.

'The one just across.'

'It's probably nothing,' said Abel.

'I heard him shaking the box,' said the woman.

The three crossed to the bungalow on the other side of the road. The snow did not retard them. Now that the men were with her, the woman led the way. Her feet were bare. She wore a tweed overcoat above her nightdress. Her hair was straight and blonde but pressed into shapely fins above her temples.

She opened her front door with a key to the Yale lock. Abel followed Lincoln up the central passage of the house. It smelled of damp carpet. A light was on in the kitchen. 'Anyone there?' called Lincoln.

The kitchen was empty.

'Did you leave this light on when you went to bed?' Abel asked the woman.

'I must've done.'

'Our time's been wasted here,' said Dorne, still playing the policeman.

'It's almost morning,' said the woman. 'Perhaps I could make some tea.'

'Tea would be nice,' said Lincoln with some degree of firmness.

23

The woman led the men to the front room of the house. Here Abel saw a carton of beer and a chair facing a window and the sea. The snow could be seen in the light escaping the room. Abel took a bottle from the open carton, removed its cap with the buckle of his belt and sat down in the chair.

'I could put up with some heat,' he said. He felt no call for politeness with this woman. Yet he had to admit that events were taking on a felicitous quality, conforming themselves to the shape of an interlude.

The woman plugged a heater in and pushed it toward Abel's feet. 'You must think me terribly silly, hysterical and that.'

'Neurotic. Possibly randy.'

'Possibly a bit, I suppose. It comes with a nervy disposition. Do you take sugar?'

Lincoln followed her back to the kitchen. The heater reddened with creakings of expansion. Abel cogitated. Few women could ignore Lincoln's assertive hips, the punch implicit between them, the way his loins were wrapped. Abel fully expected to be served the tea he had declined, but it did not arrive. He watched the snow dwindle and read the label on his bottle of beer. At length he became aware that the noises of tea-making had ceased altogether.

Abel remembered that he had seen a clock in the kitchen. He went to look at the time. Four-thirty. A jug steamed, no longer boiling. The door of an adjacent room was ajar. Abel assumed this room contained a bed. He pushed the door gently and looked beyond it. The lower halves of the lovers were exposed. While adjusting the sheet beneath the woman, Lincoln was poised on his side. His dark erection was bent toward the mattress. There seemed to be a great deal of it, from testicles to glans, considerable distance. It glinted like basted meat.

'What do you want?' asked Lincoln.

'Should you be screwing a mad person?'

'Go away.'

24

'I think I might need him, Link,' said the woman.

'I have to be at work soon,' said Abel.

'You queer cunt,' said Lincoln.

Abel went back to the chair and finished his beer. Then he rose, unplugged the heater and left the house. Leaving a keen silence, creating a great absence, the snow had stopped falling. The sky was yet unstained by any of dawn's colours. It seemed unlikely that time still operated. Abel saw that the esplanade was unchanged, that the cars and lampposts had not stirred at all, had not advanced. Over the fallen snow the orange streetlamps fanned an assortment of coppery hues. Each seemed dilute. But Abel felt omnipotent and charged, placed where he might best serve, magnanimous.

Magnanimous, yes. For some reason, magnanimous. Being himself: he felt it to be a knack.

The markets were not far.

Seven

Oranges and lemons.

Beginning at five in the morning, I worked at a produce market amid tomatoes and onions, swedes and carrots and parsnips, wet cauliflowers and big-leaved cabbages. I was a barrow boy skilled in the movement of creaking cases, of tight sacks of gourds and potatoes. Making slim holes of entry, rats liked to get inside the pumpkins. One of the Chinese growers had a homicidal temper. An insider's recollection: the heaviest sacks on the floor contained peanuts.

I was abroad in the world. Aunt Ellen was still alive. Aunt Ellen was not yet dead. I bought and studied a dictionary of psychological terms.

Between Allen and Blair Streets, George Thomas & Co and Laery & Co Ltd dwelt under the same roof. WELLINGTON PRODUCE EXCHANGE LTD was spelled plainly into the chalky concrete facade of the building. The names of Thomas and Laery might still be glimpsed, in enamel and gilt, on windows barred and darkened, bisected by interior walls or with stairs built over them. This was an old building designed to be simple: it brought the streets inside. And every morning from scratch new cities were assembled, new thoroughfares of fruit and vegetables, with little boxes and large the houses and the shops. There were mushrooms too, and flowers; I had forgotten those. On mornings in winter the loading bays were ports, the trucks streaming with an exotic rain. It was strange and pleasurable to be working at that hour, when beyond the light the road was black with drizzle. So I heaved and hefted and dragged till my torso glistened. In those days I could work: I mean by that that I could drink and drug until I was cross-eyed and still get to my place of employment. If alcohol troubled me, it also sweetened my nature. It most often troubled me when it ran out; when, in short, on any given occasion, there was no more of it. But this is not the story of my disappointment, my weakness, however permissible: this is the story of my strength, strengths, of my application of forces and skills.

The house in Lyall Bay had been abandoned. Athol was boarding with a bus-driver's widow. I slept on the floors and couches of friends. We were all unmarried. As a generation we tried hard, hard, to be tolerant and charitable. And it was so, we succeeded.

I read *King Lear* and *Under the Volcano*. What would my dictionary of psychology yield, if I still had it? Wispy pencillings and exclamation marks?

From the library's reference copy of *Banks Encyclopaedia of Psychology*, some things that catch the eye, attach themselves to my memory of Aunt Ellen:

'Schizotypal personality disorder.' 'Dysphoria.' 'Senile dementia: Alzheimer's type.' (A progression here; a darkening of shades.) 'Dysphoria' again and, 'Meacher (1972) concluded that some senile behaviour is really an adaptive response to the demands of institutional life.'

A clinician must distinguish between dementia and delirium. The dictionary next lists (in bold lower case) 'Dementia Praecox' and 'Demonic Influence and Psychopathology'. In another part of the book I learn that 'bruxism' is the grinding of the teeth in sleep. It is common in adolescents and alcoholics; it is thought to express anger, resentment.

By the time Aunt Ellen died, I was a man and Athol, too, was dead. They are buried together somewhere in Karori cemetery, in a place I remember as being a dank depression, a hollow full of blackberry and the soapy odour of fennel. Futile and cowardly to say I loved her. Accept my avowal that I would have helped her, changed her, had I had the ability.

   If summer

Eight

Blood approached his foreman and said, 'It's time I had a break.'

'Blimey. I'd forgotten about you. Off you go then, quick.'

Abel jumped down into an empty loading bay. There was warmth in the air but the sky was overcast. Abel was wearing flared, faded jeans and a khaki pullover with holes in the elbows. His hair sat in curls about his shoulders, creating an impression of blondness. The moustache was auburn, sleek and precocious, but Abel had shaved the rest of his face within the last three days. His eyes were brown with a tawny suggestion of polluted physical ripeness beneath them, feeding them. He was otherwise fresh and thin with a hint of pride in his gait, a slight wish to be noticed implicit in his stride.

Thursday, September 9, 1976. In another, remote country, Mao Tse-tung died on this date. As his broad features froze, as frost spread across them, perhaps his incommunicable longing for austerity and silence was realised. Before the month was up, Patty Hearst would be gaoled for seven years for armed robbery.

Warmth, then, and dullness; a resolved and final sky; a ceiling of cloud more grey than white with tucks and folds of bruise-coloured darkness. Continental weather, thought Abel; the stillness of Easter or national emergency. The canopy of wires above Courtenay Place was traversed by two poles, the pantographs of a red trolley bus. Pivoting slots adhering to cables: the heads of the poles seemed slickly obedient to what was oiled, receptive.

A blue, melting spark. The sizzle of fusion.

The bar Abel entered was noisy and full. A jukebox was playing, someone strummed a guitar and a chair had been overturned. Abel pushed his way through the mob to the door at the back.

Guy Ace was in the quieter, private bar. He stood at a table with a jug of beer before him. Guy's beard had an appearance of vernal immaturity or newness; its tender swirls disclosed the skin of his cheeks and neck. The tips of his moustache were taking a dihedral tilt. He was wearing a hat today, a brown one with a dark, lustrous feather. His face was a smoky lambency, a formal composition of feeble lights: his skin seemed bronzed by flame, by an old sagacity. And he seemed to look down at Abel, look *out* at Abel with a sentimental contempt for wind, for the cruelties of landscape.

'There's beer here,' he said. He was taller than Abel. This room was bright and orderly. A man Abel knew stood at the bar, a dealer in paintings, a gallery-owner. He did not seem out of place among the gentlemanly dustmen and elderly TAB clients who frequented the place. Sitting nearby was a woman Abel had not seen in the bar before. A girl, really, he thought. She had placed a rag doll on the table next to her glass and tobacco.

Ace slid a matchbox across the table to Abel. 'Two black bombers.'

'Make it four,' said Abel.

'I can't. I've thrown in four fives of Valium.'

'I'd prefer barbiturates. Valium I can get.' He handed Ace a five-dollar note.

'You can never have enough Valium,' said Ace. 'Who's the chick with the doll? I'd like to clean her teeth with my cock.'

'How gross. How indelicate. Can I have the key to the garage?'

'Of course you can have the key to the garage. I thought you *had* a key to the garage.'

'I'll get one cut today, this afternoon. I might have to use the garage all of a sudden.'

'You want to screw the chick with the doll.'

'I'm not even thinking about . . .'

'. . . the chick with the doll. Of course not.'

'I've got to go back to work.'

'Obviously.'

'What's on the agenda for you this afternoon?'

'You talk as if I'd just got up. I'm trying to track down a part for the bike. I'm told Newtown's a good place to look.' Ace put the strap of his bag across his shoulder and stepped back from the table.

'I'll see you perhaps.'

'Take care.'

When Guy Ace had gone, Abel picked up his glass and approached the girl sitting on her own. She was rolling a cigarette. 'You look like a very nice sort of person,' he said.

'I have wealthy parents. They pay me to go out and indulge myself. It keeps me away from the neighbourhood.'

'Of course. Perhaps you'd like me to buy you a drink.'

'I'm not going to the bar again. They pass remarks about my appearance.' She picked some money, a note, from her purse. 'Is this any good?'

'I'll buy us a jug,' said Abel.

He was on his way to the servery when a swift darkening of carpet and walls took place. A wand had touched the bar, imparting gloom. Abel's entrails seemed to swoon, to char and melt. His heart asserted itself with rubbery vigour.

'I think I'm drinking too much,' the art-dealer told him.

'I always work on the principle that I'm drinking too little,' said Abel.

'I take a large Scotch in order to get to sleep.'

'Try hot milk and rum.'

'Hot milk and rum. Perhaps I'll buy a bottle. My migraine's bad at night and my wife rings up. I shouldn't call her my

31

wife. She regrets the divorce and rings every night, and there I am half-sloshed. Do you think she can tell?'

'Beats me.'

'I've perverted all my liturgical instincts. If I could sell the right painting, I'd go to Spain for a month.'

'Nice there, I imagine.'

Abel took the jug the barman had filled and returned to the table at which the girl was waiting. He handed her her change, a lot of it. 'Does the doll have a name?' he asked.

'Sigmund.'

'And yours?'

'Electra. I decided to come to town today because Daddy was in the rumpus room with all the blinds down, and Mummy had gone in the roses to cut her wrists. She makes these little nicks. Daddy says you should run the blade along the vein, not saw straight across.'

'And what does he do?'

'He's a surgeon.'

'Excuse me for a jiffy,' said Abel, 'there's something I have to do.'

He felt bloodied and injured, himself, in need of a doctor's attention. Coming down from speed was like falling down a steep flight of steps, like making a grazing descent into a spiritual basement. He went to the men's and took a capsule out of the matchbox; he swallowed the Methedrine down with some water from a tap. And scooped up the water like a penitent, a pilgrim at an oasis.

Nine

He could seem to be clear-headed. He was reasonable, contrary. He shone lights through steam.

My brother's plans were always the most economical descriptions of ways to avoid being paid, do business in a vacuum.

The undersides of his arms were pale, his throat hirsute and white.

Conrad grew up to be moderately tall, pleasingly lean. His dry, black hair was browned by a lustre – like that of rusty oil. The kind, Irish darkness of his eyes would be heightened when he blushed, would be given a teasing glitter of concentration, and he blushed when he ordered meals or asked the simplest questions, when buying tickets or explaining himself to others. Yet he could put his case unflinchingly. His hands and wrists were broad, issued him from some deep genetic bag. He lacked timidity and could not conserve himself; he lacked discrimination in his sexual conduct. And blundered, tolerantly. He regretted things belatedly and grinned, making more friendly phone calls, arrangements. Difficulties and people yielded to him – and there he was again, knee-deep in broken eggs while inwardly recumbent, apologetic but somewhat edified, at home in confusion.

But he was cooler than me, always more free and uncaring of conventions, of others' inhibitions. I might be contemptuous of their tasteless pictures and worthless ornaments, but Conrad was aloof to other people's edges, their borders, their areas of exclusion. And he moved like a ghost through systems of belief. He moved through religions like the Invisible Man: from Zen to Egyptology, an ethereal passage. I could not see that he profited by this; he returned empty-handed, as if immune to enrichment. Nor did he want, after all, to too much complicate himself.

The tense I'm using is not meant to imply his imminent desertion of my story. And I speak of him as we agree he was, often at rest, often doing something with his fingers to an electric toaster or a mechanical toy, setting things back on track, putting things right, for the moment. (This little train of his enterprise has too much zestful sting, will soon derail.) But he was tall and adult, slight-buttocked, long-lashed and unshaven when he met me for drinks in those days, as he so often did. To say that he mistook

Ten

Having made the acquaintance of Electra and her doll, Abel went back to the market. Hundreds of cases of bananas arrived. They were put into coolers to ripen, stacked in darkness and fed a gas, a sweet gas which yellowed them.

Abel finished work feeling weak and transparent, jumpy but talkative. His mouth was dry and his triceps ached; his mind had a brittle momentum, a craving for something that had not yet announced itself. The sun was low and blue, a bleak source of warmth. He walked to Willis St through the friendly congestion of a Friday afternoon, the dry exhalations of shops, sometimes leather-scented. Night would bring drizzle, perhaps, lay a porous gloss on the streets.

The public bar of the Grand Hotel was populous, welcoming. It was a spacious place, carpeted and mirrored, its servery an island. Abel bought a jug of beer and a double vodka and orange. His brother sat on a stool at a high table. 'I'm broke,' said Conrad.

'There's a full jug here.'

'I need money. I think I should go to Auckland. A change of scene would get my juices going, shake me from my lethargy a bit.'

'There's nothing wrong with your juices.'

'I wish I was more like him.'

'The bloke with the tonsure?'

'Looks like a broken-down actor, an athlete gone to fat. You can still see the old polish.'

As if remotely attuned to their conversation, the man in

question looked toward the Bloods, his gaze uninterested, fortuitous.

'He can't possibly hear us,' said Conrad.

'I bet he's a cop.'

'A wrestler.'

The man stood on his own some distance away, his glass on a leaner beside him. His fawn trench coat was open. He wore a pink shirt without a tie. Nothing about his dress seemed particularly clean. Abel formed an impression of subtle decline, of deviation from some standard, former profession or office. The man had great thoracic bulk. Abel saw too that the bald head detracted from the youthfulness of the face. The man's black eyebrows had an adolescent fineness, an expression of slight regret or apology.

'Should we invite him over?' asked Conrad.

'Do what you like.' It was that sort of pub.

Abel went to the servery for another vodka. Resisting the urge to take any more Methedrine was becoming a conscious priority. The worst would start at around midnight; the signals of deprivation might begin their shrill agitation, but he would be drunk by then. He had no wish to feel the sure retreat of the drug from his veins.

He bought Conrad a whisky. As he waited for his change he glanced to his right. On the servery lay a doll wearing a red Tyrolean cap.

'Hello again,' said Electra.

'You get around,' said Abel. He lifted his drinks from the mat on which they had stood.

'I've been playing the piano in a bar near here. A journalist bought me Kahlua.'

'I'm with my brother.'

'Just tripping from bar to bar, that's me. I rang Daddy. Mummy's gone to bed with the dog.'

'There's been no more bloodshed?'

'Touch wood. It's grim just the same.'

'You'd better bring Sigmund.'

'Is your brother the long one?'

Abel led her to the table at which the balding man had joined Conrad. 'Ah. Don't know your name. I'm Abel. This, I think, is Electra.'

'I'm Conrad.'

'And my name's Omar Kidd.'

The table seemed suddenly laden with drinks, with embarrassments and timid expectations. Electra raised a glass full of a pink confection.

'Here's cheers,' said Conrad, grateful for the whisky.

Kidd eyed Electra. 'I was up the road and happened to hear you playing.'

'Chopin,' said Electra.

'His cool nostalgic lights.'

'He's all I can remember in certain moods.'

'And did you study formally?'

'Not much. I puddle about till I get things right. Mummy's the one with the training.'

'You deserve a better piano,' said Kidd. His voice had something glottal in it. This tonal rotundity had passed through an eloquent darkness – it issued from a cathedral of a chest. Abel reflected that Conrad had been right: Kidd had an actor's voice, one almost irrelevant to life and advancement.

'And you play too?' Abel asked him.

'Alas, not at all. One of my Vietnamese friends, an officer I was advising, had quite a knowledge of the French repertoire.'

'You made a friend in Vietnam?' asked Conrad.

Kidd was silent for a moment. He stared into the glass of beer he held. Then he looked across the bar toward the door, returned his gaze to Conrad and rolled his jaw. 'Am I mistaken in thinking I was *asked* to drink at this table?'

'Of course not,' said Abel.

'A national communism,' Conrad said. 'There's no sullying that, though Dulles tried.'

'It wasn't as simple as you seem to think,' said Kidd.

'A dutiful Catholic, was he, this friend of yours?'

'The word dutiful is not one I associate with the Vietnamese.'

'Bloody Catholics.'

'You're one yourself,' said Abel. Conrad, he reflected, was not much of a drinker. The younger Blood finished his whisky and turned his attention to Electra.

'What's a big girl like you doing with a doll?'

'You sound so jealous, Conrad. Often the broadest minds are the most conventional. Sigmund's nice. He's lucky. I rescued him from a bin.'

'Pretend I'm in a bin.'

'Shall I buy you another whisky? Can you go the bar on your own?'

Kidd addressed Abel. 'My friend was killed eventually,' he murmured.

'War.'

'Bloody bloody arrogance and meddling, of the most cynical kind. Your brother's right.'

'Don't let him hear that. What are you doing with yourself at present?'

Kidd looked away again, down the length of the bar and back to the glass in his hand, the beer he seemed not to want very much. 'I find myself at a very loose end indeed.'

Eleven

Conrad returned to the table with another glass of froth for Electra. Between her and Kidd, the talk reverted to shy appreciations of music. They touched on César Franck, Henri Duparc, Debussy and Saint-Saëns. Electra was wearing a straight muslin dress stintingly embroidered about the hem and cuffs. For warmth she had covered her shoulders with a cardigan depicting the stone molars and cylindrical eyes of an Inca mosaic, a tessellation of browns and blacks and reds. Her brassière and panties were visible through her dress. And her brown skin. When I shifted Sigmund from the top of the table to a lower, drier shelf, I saw that she and my brother were holding hands. Sigmund looked at me with plastic eyes that seemed to know hilarity.

'Who's coming up the road?' Conrad asked the company. 'What's the attraction?'

'I thought if you were slumming, my girl — do people slum anymore? — you might want to see the Duke before it closes.'

'And find a party? Let's.'

'Omar?' bullied Conrad.

'My flat's very close.' Kidd's voice had found a new depth. 'I thought Abel might fancy a chat.' He looked at me as if expecting disappointment. Had he been a homosexual, his interest would have been in Conrad.

I glanced at my watch. 'It's only just gone eight,' I said to Conrad. 'Perhaps I'll catch you later.'

We left the hotel as a group. 'I've enjoyed myself, Mr Kidd,' Electra said in the street. As she went off with Conrad, their holding of hands suspended, Sigmund's startled face yawed between their legs.

It had been raining. The sky was a muddy pink. Across the street was a building whose awning had a wrought-iron fringe. (I think of the city as a place of points, of spires and filigrees.) A taxi squished suspiciously to a halt. Omar Kidd and I began to walk. My senses are at their coolest, my emotions most ordered, when I move through the wet city. Heating the basest metals, our memories of our earliest impressions, we each uniquely decoct *nostalgia* in our hearts (I must have a word to apply to those sweet thoughts the glazed streets engender). Rain falls through all that great wealth of air, cloaking all the buildings – and human artefacts seem erstwhile, eternal. I feel pacific, justly abated. The city bathes me. It seems to represent an elaborate sadness, a thing of many layers and stony aspects, architectural saucers and bowls, all receptive of drizzle. Being so very old, the city is lachrymose. And I feel deeply edified and muted, richly supplied with a bland identity.

Perhaps Kidd's flat was lodged in a shaft, a perpendicular fault in the city's clay. We climbed steps to it, a steep municipal flight. An artificial light fell on the wet concrete. Later, it was never entirely clear to me where I had gone that night, what mushroom-coloured cell I'd penetrated. I remember a view of a spray of lights, the black lake of the harbour. His kitchen was the room Kidd seemed to favour. Some moribund red roses lay on a sheet of newspaper, ready to be wrapped and disposed of. On the bench and table were many jars and cans of imported foods. I saw smoked oysters and duck in orange sauce. Kidd's calendar was five years out of date. If he cooked at all, he cooked on a gas stove. On the low refrigerator stood a Gestetner machine.

'Sit down at the table. The other room's a shambles. I'm glad of an excuse to stop drinking beer. Can I offer you some of this?'

Kidd showed me a bottle with a spoon in the neck: I

volunteered to drink what remained of the red wine. He filled a glass tankard with water from the tap and joined me at the table. I was made aware of the breadth of his face, his gaze. There were flecks of black in his brown eyes.

'If you want to smoke you'll have to use a saucer.' He pushed one toward me. Then he looked around the room, panning it with his wide face. He seemed to want to explain his apparent poverty, the chill in his kitchen. He had not removed his coat. 'I live on my wits, now more than ever. I once belonged to a group. For all the good we did, we might as well have collected teaspoons. Two of us had been overseas defending one sort of economic system, expanding it. We had gazed into the fire. I used to edit a little magazine and do my bit of recruiting. I sometimes wondered what I belonged to, to whom. Then we had a chap try to bomb a certain building. Our SIS was meeting some vicious American. Our bloke had always wanted to bomb something. Futile, he knew, but there it was. You will have read of a car exploding outside a bakery.'

I had. I had also seen pictures of the sooty wreckage.

'An empty Wellington street. A Sunday, slightly wet. The man blown to pieces trying to place that bomb – I have his file in this flat, his photograph and a list of his skills.'

'Is that quite wise?'

'It doesn't matter. There's nothing left of the group. I see in you a reckless innocence, a restiveness amounting to a weakness. It makes me ill to look at your pupils. I saw eyes like yours at Hue. Tell me, have you ever been in trouble with the police.'

'No.'

'Do you hold a passport.'

'No.'

A long-bodied fruit-fly began to trouble Kidd. Perhaps it had come from the tropics, an agent of delirium and confession. I remembered the roses in the room, the edges of their petals blackening. Kidd waved away the iridescent fly, its batty manoeuvrings. From beneath the pamphlets and bills heaped at the end of the table, he drew a small Minolta. 'From time to time I need a courier. I might, for instance, at some future date, offer you money for taking some item north.'

'My interest in politics is entirely academic. I'm too much of a pessimist to think . . .'

'The business I propose would be purely criminal, merely illegal. Your participation would depend on how much you wanted the money.'

'On my greed, in other words.'

'You'd do the job on the understanding that you remained ignorant of what you transported. I'd give you ten minutes' training on how to spot surveillance. Do you mind if I take your picture?'

'Of course I mind.'

'Forgive me. Old habits. Once I'd have sat up at night doing my bit of typing, doing my bit for the cause, trimming your picture and pasting it on a card.'

Twelve

I was free of Methedrine by the following Monday. Accept the claims I make; embrace what I tell you. I'd slept in the garage on the mattress I kept there, in the bulky shadow of Guy Ace's Triumph. The hum of the world was absent from that garage. Ace had contrived a supply of electricity. Darkness without: the webby four-paned window reflected the caged bulb he had rigged up. I boiled the jug, made myself some coffee, took the last of my Valium from the matchbox, the two five-milligram tablets I'd been hoarding, and swallowed them with a sip of the sweet black coffee.

I went to work as usual. Daybreak was a streaming of soiled clouds before the first gale of spring. I waited until late in the morning to slip away up Blair St. The key-cutter's shop was a dark cubicle. I had a copy of the key to the garage made and returned the original to Guy in the pub. When I got back to the market, the pleasant operation of sweeping its vast floor was ahead of me. Gesticulating commerce had been replaced by layers of dusty light and empty space.

There was in those days, close to the huddle of buildings that house the *Evening Post*, a restaurant that served a plump deep-fried sausage, crumbed, with gravy, chips and a salad. Sauces were left on the tables, Worcestershire and tomato. A room near the kitchen offered carpet, a prototypical Muzak, creamy-sanded Greece as a holiday destination. I was finishing an evening meal when Freddie West approached my table. The dealer in paintings and reputations sat down across from me. 'You've got circles under your eyes. Arcs. I wonder if I have.'

'Not so's you'd notice,' I said.

'I took your advice and bought a bottle of rum. I found it very seductive, moreish. When my wife rang up I told her my companions were Elgar and Britten.'

'Good for you.'

'My migraine's much improved in spite of the milk. Elaine has undertaken to ring me only once a week.'

'Perhaps that's it.'

'Perhaps that's what?'

'The lessening of stress has made your headaches less frequent.'

'Migraine is to the brain what gout is to the toe, my doctor says.'

'And cured by death no doubt. Would you like some of my chips?'

'The oysters here are very good,' said West. 'I need taking out of myself.'

'Have you been into the Foresters' Arms?'

'I saw that chap who urinates under tables. I've never cared for the look of him. Anyway, I'm trying to stay out of hotels.'

I was, of course, a lot younger than West. In spite of our having a number of mutual friends, I was flattered by his awareness of me. I thought it remarkable that he should speak to me as often as he did, but our paths kept crossing. I would see his leather coat across a room and anticipate his frown of complicity and greeting. His dry, blond mass of curls seemed to magnify the movements of his head. He had the square, creased features of a certain type of boxer, a pug whose cheeks are often cut and marred in the healing.

'I suppose you've seen enough of pictures for the day,' I said.

'I'm showing Ivan Strange at the moment. Don't you read the papers?'

'Is he the one who does those sections of viscera in tin?'

'It's as if one is looking through a hole in muscle.'

'Not like you to be at a loose end,' I said, pushing my empty plate toward the waitress. 'I'm going to buy a bottle and take it somewhere to drink. Perhaps I could show you a couple of things.'

We took a taxi from the Bond St rank. After a day of wind and flashes of sunshine, of sheets of paper riding the air like gulls and empty cans being skipped along the gutters, Mount Victoria was enjoying the calm of exhaustion. Freddie West showed little surprise when I opened a door in the larger door of the garage, crouched, stepped inside and beckoned him to follow.

'A hot piece of real estate,' he said when we both stood erect again. The gloom was brought to the level of a dusk, a mellow botanical twilight, by the window's chalky panes. West stroked the seat of Ace's taurine Triumph. I took the bottle I'd bought over to the bench against the wall, selected two of the cleanest plastic cups and set about pouring some rum. Freddie sat down in the veteran armchair Guy had saved from a journey to the tip (dragging it to safety down the street at midnight).

'Guy Ace pays the rent. You must have seen him about.'

'It has its points, I suppose.' West picked at the hole in the chair's armrest, thought better of this behaviour and stopped.

I handed him a cup. 'No milk in this, I'm afraid.'

'I lied about drinking it with milk.' He really was the ideal guest.

He drank. I plugged in the mechanic's lamp suspended from a beam above the bench. Then I stooped beneath the bench, lifted the sheet of calico from the art boards stored there and brought the first board up into the light, propping it on the bench to face Freddie.

'I don't much care for work in polymers.' He looked for a moment, thinking. 'That's fluid, adroit enough. He draws with his brush. I take it he's a he.'

'The only clue I'll allow you.'

'Show me the next.'

I brought the second painting up and stood it in front of the first. 'There are some inventive passages,' said West. 'I'm guessing your man is an autodidact.'

'Not quite. He did some design at the Polytech.'

'That's worse. It coarsens a gifted painter. There's more of an allusion here to Bacon. Perhaps he takes his figures too directly from André François. Still, I like his palette. Can he work in oils?'

'He was stretching some twelve-ounce cotton duck when I last saw him.'

'Good.'

When I had shown Freddie the three remaining pictures, he stood and gave me his cup. I charged it with rum again. He put on spectacles and peered at the surface of the last of the paintings. Then he straightened and took his cup from my hand. 'Are you going to tell me who the painter is?' In the light from the bulb above, his glasses threw golden wedges down his cheeks.

'His name is Conrad Blood.'

'He's versatile.'

'He's a worry.'

'Yet *you* live in a garage.'

'Not *live* exactly.'

West removed his glasses and settled once more in the decrepit armchair. 'I'd like to say I'll represent your brother, but I have to know how hard he works.' He drank from his cup as if finding its contents agreeable. 'There's been little hardship in my adult life. I formed very early the intention of making money, of getting even. I'd make up for my father's poverty. Yet I'm full of all sorts of angers and resentments, I punish myself with fiery bouts of migraine. I'm not so very different from that chicken-farmer with the withered leg, Hitler's propagandist, Doctor Goebbels. I fear, I hate, I scurry away from conflict. In my youth I thought I was being called to the priesthood. That's not so very laughable, perhaps. The paintings I handle daily are the trappings of a liturgy, the furnishings of an altar. I have the habits of a parish priest. Is it safe to smoke in here?'

'Probably not.'

Freddie produced a packet of Camels, put a cigarette between his lips and lit a match. He seemed to bathe his face in the yellow flame he held in his cupped hands.

'From time to time,' he said, 'I feel the need to give, to help, to be larger than I am. You strike me as being more than usually bright, in a fucked-up kind of way. That makes you attractive. I own a house near a river. Lying in the scrub beside a pool is the wreck of a DC-3. Butterflies and mushrooms abound. And though it rains a lot it's always warm. From any part of the house you can hear the surf. I bought it for a song when I was about your age. It needed fixing, it needed propping up, it needed, in short, salvation. I'd drive along Pa Road with timber on the roof of my Morris, on my way to my ruin of a house. It might be of use to you or Conrad.'

Thirteen

On Tuesday afternoon Abel walked to Aro St. The seasonal winds had dropped. Warmth issued from gates and walls at the level of his thighs. The tars streaking the surface of the road seemed to reflect the blueness of the sky. Some crushed camellia blooms lay along the bottom of a fence. A stopcock lacked its lid. The air was made weedy and green by the stench of a hydrangea bush, but Conrad's door was in sunlight. He rented a narrow house with sides of corrugated iron.

Electra greeted Abel.

'That brother of mine about?'

The front room of the cottage had a varnished floor. Toi-toi stood in a glazed ceramic flagon on the hearth of the fireplace. Abel sat down on the couch beneath the window.

'He's making his spaghetti bolognaise, whispered of from here to I don't know where.'

Conrad came in through a curtain of stout beads. At the window, wind-chimes stirred. 'Hi. I'm stoned. It's taken me an hour to find the colander.' He took a cigarette from a packet on the mantelpiece. Under the grey stuff of his T-shirt, his stomach was a shallow concavity.

'I was talking to Freddie West,' Abel said.

'Who's he?'

'Freddie West of West Gallery. At least make an effort.'

'I've got to stir the sauce. They call it a sauce. What did he want?'

'Oh, you know. He expressed a bit of an interest in your work.'

'Anyone got a light?'

'He was offering a place for you to paint in.'

'I can paint anywhere. Or *not* paint anywhere, as the case may be.'

Conrad found a box of matches and returned with it to the kitchen. Electra handed Abel a glass of wine. They talked of the herbs she was beginning to grow on the bank at the back of the house. The coarse pile of the fabric of the couch was hot where the sun struck it.

'Will you stay for some spaghetti?'

'Of course.'

'He won't like your having shown his paintings.'

'Don't you believe it.'

Conrad reappeared with his fists full of cutlery. Soon Abel was handed a steaming plate of food. He made room for it on the low table before him. Electra refilled his glass. Then his hosts sat down in their respective chairs, their plates perched on their knees. 'This is the life,' said Conrad.

'You need a proper table.'

'So what did you show this West, this parasite?'

'I showed him *Faun and Phallus* and *Sparks and Stars*. All the things you've left in Guy's garage.'

'I must bring them here, now I've got a place.'

'You've been here for months.'

Cars passed in the street behind Abel. He listened to the transient adhesion of tyres to the surface of the road.

'This place he suggests I paint in – in the reaches of what distant swamp does it nestle?'

'Why not ask him? You've seen him at parties, you know where his gallery is. He expressed an interest in becoming your dealer.'

'Now *that* sounds promising,' said Electra.

'I didn't put enough salt in this,' said Conrad.

Electra was the last to finish eating; Abel was helping Conrad do the dishes when she entered the kitchen, kissed Conrad's ear and went out into the yard to water her plants.

Abel dried his hands and stood in the kitchen door. Half the yard was in shadow. Electra was playing water on the bed of soil above a low wall. 'Further up – can you see? – I'm trying for tomatoes. Already there's little globes, toy fruit like jade or soap.' The fan of spray from the hose she held seemed to sustain a spectrum's airy stairs, a series of steps from red to violet.

The front room was cooler: the sun had moved. Abel sat down on the couch again. Conrad returned a twist of silver foil to a bowl on the mantelpiece. Then he lit the joint he had in his mouth. Excess paper burned, becoming ash. The almost invisible flame of the match seemed to melt the air above it. Conforming his lips to the shape of an embouchure, Conrad sucked in smoke with a whistling of saliva. He handed the joint to Abel. Abel smoked; some seconds passed. Conrad selected a record from the stack leaning against the skirting-board. He slid the LP from its cover and eased it out of its transparent sleeve, seeming to know the weight of these things. He placed the record on a turntable sunk in plywood, set the thing in slow, soundless motion and prepared to drop the stylus on a specific track.

Abel watched all this in awe. 'You've found a very beautiful companion.'

'I'd like to buy her a piano,' said Conrad.

'Of course. Quite right. A piano.'

'One with black and white keys.'

The syllables of Conrad's speech seemed loaded, weighted. They pivoted and fell, and Abel with them. He became deeply conscious of his palate, his heavy and conspicuous eyebrows. He felt a slight anxiety relating to the largeness of his teeth, his many teeth and very singular tongue. He felt he must somehow animate his face – and found himself yawning. Music began with a chord of startling concentration and freshness, of elemental burgeon (a crust was being broken), like the sun coming out or a clear wave breaking. Abel was immersed for a time in

the act of hearing, in the slow apprehension of sound. A dense, august male voice began to sing, to speak tunefully: it filled the room with intelligence, with the operation of an exterior mind, hygienic and assertive.
And everything emptying into white.
'Jesus,' said Abel.
He relinquished the joint to Conrad. On the table near Abel's shins lay Sigmund the doll, his green jerkin lewd, his eyebrow plainly cocked. Abel had not seen the telephone before. Next to it stood the chromium-plated statuette of an aeroplane. Its wings and fuselage were plump, apparently distended but sleek, and attached by an attenuated fin to a base representing the northern hemisphere.
'There's butterflies and things near Freddie's house.'
'Shut up about Freddie's house.' Conrad was flicking through his albums. 'Would you like to hear the soundtrack from *Ben Hur*?'
'Wow.'
'I'm sorry. We haven't got it.'
Like the thrill of a heart attack, Abel surmised, disappointment galvanised much of his left arm. He made the gristle and sinews of his neck perform a labour of erection and extension: now he could see his brother properly. 'I suppose you think it's funny asking that.'
'Pour yourself another glass of wine.' Conrad looked briefly like Sean Connery.
'Saying you'll . . . Offering to . . .' This dark conversation must be abandoned. Abel withdrew through a tumult of smoking swords.
'Here's something I haven't played in a while.'
'I see you have a telephone,' said Abel.
'Electra had it connected.'
The memory of an intention stirred in Abel. He had meant to make up his mind about a certain proposal. His current alert and cheerful intoxication should not prevent him bringing

the matter forward, exposing it to the light of the present moment. A telephone was handy, as idle as himself. The world was just a phone call away. From this room could be extended an instantaneous, electronic bridge emerging in New York or London. What harm in a local call?

Somewhere in his jacket he had a card. He felt for it and found it. It proved to be blank apart from a pencilled number, faint against the gloss of the board. The hand that had written it down made continental sevens. Abel dialled the number with stiff precision. At the other end of the line, the handset was lifted. There was a pause, itself resonant, the pouring rush of silence made audible. Then Omar Kidd identified himself.

Fourteen

And thus the trapdoor dropped. I had tripped it myself. I fell into a bright and brittle place. Where all reflective surfaces were black.

As to the capricious Conrad Blood – do you feel you know him any better?

Of course not.

My question implies a supposition of difference, variety. But don't we all become alike, growth implying a slavish mimesis? A child is raised in a kennel, ignored or abused as the case may be, starved or fed on scraps (use your imagination) and then at a certain age is liberated. Is she not much like us, ten years later? Has she not learned to read the paper and use lipstick? A boy who glimpsed Auschwitz at the age, say, of eight (work enough for the eyes for a hundred years) would now, if he'd survived, be only . . . fifty-two, shaving every day and going to movies.

Sometimes I dream. The protracted exertion of a futile sobriety ends for the day in sleep, if I'm in luck. And on the edge of sleep I sometimes enjoy the dreamy delusion that my few remaining friends are really all the same person; that A and B are merging into C, that they have all the time been sharing the one, hidden identity.

I hear your question. I live above a shop, what was once a shop and will be again when I have moved on, when the slithering of junk mail and bills addressed to unknown previous tenants has finally driven me out. (The TV licence-fee people mount a particularly subtle and galling campaign. How adeptly they rile the gunman in me.) Downstairs behind the shop are a kitchen and grim bathroom. Up here, well, I use a single room. I have a view of a brick-walled yard which seldom gets the sun. But through the fire-escape outside the window crowds the topmost foliage of some kind of bush or tree, undaunted by the dankness of the wall it grows against. Sometimes a tabby cat patrols the fire-escape, nosing leaves of the very palest green. I raise the window and feed it bits of mince.

What would you see, looking in from the fire-escape? Opportunity, here, for frankness and brevity. Opposite the window you would see an open door and the rail at the top of the stairs. Within the room there is light, the light of a fine afternoon in the city. You would see a tidy bed, a radio, the spines of a dozen books. The carpet has a floral pattern, drab. You would see a card-table on which sits a typewriter. The typewriter is a small manual, an old portable job with its metal finished in red, a novelty. Though it has probably been dropped out of helicopters, this hardy Smith Corona remains unbent, its mechanism fluid and unobstructive.

I write with a pen on pads I buy from Deka: even as you read, I'm writing this. And I've charged myself with the task of changing the subject, of turning an impetuous clock backward, of living again where I have no wish to be, where the least reproachful shadow inspires regret.

'It's Abel Blood,' I write, rendering my own incautious speech: I have just rung Omar Kidd from my brother's flat.

'Hello again,' said Kidd.

'I fancy a bit of a trip.'

'Good.'

'I was thinking of leaving soon.'

'And very wise, Abel. I'd like to be allowed to see you off. Perhaps we could meet tomorrow morning.'

'Name the place.'

'I'll look for you outside the railway station. Would nine o'clock suit you?'

Fifteen

The sky was solid and close, a dirty lambency seeming to muster and trap the lights of the city beneath it. And lights burned late that morning. It rained as Abel waited inside the porch, between sandy columns of yellow stone. Around the raised lawns and beds of pansies before him, the kerbs of glossy brick looked cold and slippery. A black taxi waited at the rank. As the last of the commuters from the trains hurried toward the city, their feet crossed the asphalt in front of the station. Abel saw umbrellas and coloured women's coats dimly reflected there. The pink flagstones beyond seemed to bubble and quake in the gentle inundation.

The rain made a pervasive, muted tinkling. Abel was at home on the planet. But he also felt overhung, both brittle and insubstantial, at a slight remove from responsibility.

A cab with misty panes pulled in behind the first. Omar Kidd got out of the vehicle, drew his coat around his body and climbed the few steps to the shelter of the porch. 'I trust I find you well,' he said. The words came straight from his roomy chest. He wore a grey shirt with a pattern of little roses.

'How much are you offering?' asked Abel.

Kidd took Abel's elbow and turned him toward the interior of the station. 'Four hundred dollars. Payable when you get back. I'll give you, now, a further hundred dollars for expenses.'

'That seems reasonable.'

'You'll need a ticket to Levin. Crime capital of the country, and I can't be seen there.'

They crossed the compass rose laid out in strips of brass on the floor of the building. 'How many years will I do if I get caught?' asked Abel.

'I haven't given it much thought. Nor should you.'

Though he seldom boarded trains, the concourse of the station was a part of Abel's knowledge of his city. The odour of dung suggested itself. This was an arena from which the animals had vanished: as often as he walked beneath this ceiling of tarnished glass, he caught the whiff of a zoo.

'I'd like to see you buy that ticket,' said Kidd. 'I want you in Levin by noon tomorrow.'

Kidd hung back. Abel went to the ticket window. There was a suitable train. An oblong of stiff card was slid toward him.

'I'm on my way,' he reported.

'Splendid,' said Kidd. 'Feel like a bite to eat?'

They went to the cafeteria. Steam hung over the bainsmarie. Kidd paid for their pies and cups of tea. They sat down at a table near doors of bevelled glass. Kidd reached into the pocket inside his coat and placed an envelope beside Abel's plate. 'Your money. First instalment.'

'Ta.'

Kidd's pie was covered with a thick gravy. He took up his knife and fork and cut into the bulging pastry. 'These things are good,' he said. 'Here's a pea, look.'

Abel stirred the tea in his sturdy cup.

'Now I want you to listen carefully,' said Kidd. 'Your contact works for an upholstery firm, a little place at the southern end of town called BD Buck and Sons. *His* name is Brian Winslow. He'll have a description of you as you are at this moment, so don't go changing your clothes or dyeing your hair.'

'What colour are my eyes?'

Kidd managed a smile. 'When does your train leave?'

'At ten in the morning.'

'You'll board it with a bag, an ordinary leather bag for delivery to Winslow. I'll entrust the bag to you as we leave here.' He conveyed a forkful of pie to his mouth. As he chewed he began to look troubled. Two simple pleats of worry cleft his forehead. Disdaining any emphasis he said, 'I suppose it goes without saying that your failure to deliver the bag would have the nastiest possible consequences for yourself . . . as nasty as you can imagine.'

'Of course.'

'I'm glad you understand that.' Kidd's eyes seemed unrelieved and full of woe.

'And how will I spot surveillance?'

'If you're being followed at any time, it will be by someone moving ahead of you.' Kidd smiled for the second time. 'You haven't touched your pie.'

'Too early in the day for me.'

'Sheer waste. It's time we moved.'

Abel took the envelope from the table, folded it and slipped it into the hip-pocket of his jeans. He followed Kidd out of the cafeteria and across the concourse. Above the platforms to the left, cloud seemed to touch the rooves of carriages. Spent rain, bright and cold, lay along the tops of the rails. Ahead of the listless trains was a long island of mist, green bodies of water and dipping fences, of fogs darkened by the shapes of crippled manuka. At the Left Luggage office, Kidd tendered a receipt. The attendant returned from his search of the orderly shelves with a brown bag. Abel took it down from the counter.

'You happy now?' asked Kidd.

'I don't know, Uncle, what I'd have done without you,' Abel said for the attendant's benefit.

Outside the office Kidd said, 'Ring me when you get back.'

They shook hands then. Kidd's grip was powerful. 'I'll put the goods somewhere safe,' said Abel.

'I won't ask where. But have a quiet day.'

'I'll try.'

'Don't disappoint me, Abel. Don't.'

Sixteen

There were ridges of water that trembled, broke and sprang in gleaming forks down the surface of the windshield. The taxi ponged of drying wool. I rode to a corner near the garage and paid the cabby off. Inside the garage I made coffee, lit a cigarette and sank into the armchair. I stretched myself in the dimness, the only light the glow from the rain-spattered window. The pale stalks of weeds pressed at its panes like flesh. Perhaps my mood was one of melancholic calm: I enjoyed a sheltered anonymity. The bag sat on the bench. It was of the type that men carry flagons in (or sports gear or tools), with a zip along the top, short straps for handles and two semi-circular decorative tabs stitched to the panels at either end – you know the sort. My custody of it mocked my many hollow principles; I looked at it and wondered what degree of risk it represented.

I heard Guy Ace arrive, coast his Triumph up on the pavement outside and set it on its stand with a heave. I let him in and watched him remove his gauntlets. 'This better be important,' he said.

'I have a bag. It's there on the bench. I want to know what it contains.'

Guy took the bag to the window. 'See for yourself,' he said. 'Toothpaste. Soap. Minties.'

'No, no. I mean *really* contains.'

'You think there's something hidden in here?'

'In the lining perhaps. At the bottom somehow.'

Guy hung his mechanic's lamp above the bench. I plugged it in and he had light. His face had a look of repose, of engagement in a task. He emptied the bag of its contents and began to examine its interior.

I had, of course, arranged that he should come. He had a skill I needed, not the skill he was exercising with knife and pliers, but his talent for moving forward nervelessly. With small and cautious movements of his fingers, of his tongue between wet lips, he seemed to engage some gift for penetration.

Within fifteen minutes the bag was gutted; Guy had lifted the bottom out of it. The materials of my life had been rearranged.

Imagine things laid out; imagine things to hand, and then . . . The subtle disorder of newness.

'I'd say it's heroin,' Guy said.

We were looking at a broad, flat sachet. Like a flat, compacted bag of icing-sugar.

Seventeen

Sunlight was snatched away. The carriage entered a tunnel. There was violence in the event, the gust of collision avoided. Abel imagined he heard a snatch of hellish singing. He moved like a scarlet dot across a map, a small, pulsing beacon signalling a journey. And the headlines in his paper, the *Evening Post* of the previous day, consolidated his sense of his own weird folly: 'All Hope Gone For Antarctic Team', 'Samoan Prince Felt Slighted In Britain'.

The platform at Levin was an end to undulation. It slid into place with precision, seeming to come to meet Abel's window. He took up the bag from the seat beside him and left the train. Cultivated fields were close; he could smell them in the air above the sunny station. The diffident breeze contained the scent of that dry warmth between rows of plants, of loam, manure and desiccated soil.

He walked along to the toilet at the end of the platform. As he washed his face in cold water and ran a comb through his hair, Abel heard a graunching of steel. When he emerged from the toilet, he saw that the train was moving out.

Above the glare of the rails and the hot gravel, a trio of cabbage whites struggled witlessly. Some poplars stood on the other side of the track; a silver ripple moved through their leaves like smoke. Beyond the flat and patterned shelf of the land, mountains rose like brittle novelties, their preponderant mass made tractable by distance. Snow caked their highest parts.

A porter wheeled a barrow laden with parcels into the shadow of the station's awning. Abel knew himself to be at the southern end of town. His wristwatch showed that it was only a few minutes after eleven, but Abel hoped to address the situation, to hasten his release from responsibility. He crossed the highway and began to walk north.

The cloudless sky seemed weightless. Abel passed a wide paddock with a cenotaph at its corner. With most of the town as yet ahead of him, next to a yard with caravans for sale he found the building he sought. It was clad with weather-boards that had never been painted, now bleached and worn to a smoothness, a littoral greyness. Its piles were visible. Like that of an old pub, its entrance faced the intersection of two pavements. The sign along the side of the building read, BD BUCK & SONS.

Abel mounted three wooden steps.

'It's warming up a bit,' said the man inside the door. He had a pencil behind his ear.

'Is Brian Winslow about?' The workshop was dark and quiet.

'I've got an idea he's out. He goes to that pub up the road.'

The hotel was a block away. Entering the public bar, Abel felt more than ever aware of the bag he carried. A group of men in singlets stood around a table. An older man in a monogrammed blazer was drinking at the counter. Abel bought a seven-ounce beer and asked for Brian, a Brian, an upholsterer perhaps.

'That's him by the door,' said the barman. 'What's he done?'

At the end of the bar was a young man in overalls, a glass of whisky or rum in front of him. Unshaven, dark, he yet looked nervous, ill.

Abel approached him and said, 'I'm up from Wellington.'

'Oh?'

'I've got some samples with me. You expressed an interest.'

'Of course. Them new fabrics.' He spoke as if bored, depressed. 'Do you mind if we do this bullshit in the car?'

They swallowed their respective drinks. Then Abel followed

61

Winslow into the street. The car was a dilapidated heap, a Falcon painted in patches of blue and grey, chalky and washed out. 'Hop in,' said Winslow. 'You'll have to shift that nonsense off the seat.'

Abel moved a few things to the floor – a Stanley knife, a road-map – and seated himself with the bag on his lap. With its doors closed and windows up, the car was a place of retreat and privacy.

'She's good on the highway. I give her heaps.' Winslow took a flask of whisky from the glove compartment.

'She seems sound enough.' Abel looked out at the stationary pub, the curtained window of a Chinese restaurant.

'This business we're in, this business we're doing – any idea how it works?'

'Who's up who and who's not paying? No.'

'You're doing it to see if you can do it.'

He drank from the flask and extended it to Abel. Abel tasted the whisky, disliked it but drank again. They might have been parked in a town in America, the meeting-place of farmer and salesman, with shining tractors on show in the heat of noon.

'I like it here in winter,' Winslow said, taking the flask from Abel. 'I like the look of rain at night, on a lawn in the light from a door. I guess it feeds the fucking worms. Did you ever see that film with Frank Sinatra? He's driving along in a downpour. He kills himself by turning his wipers off. There's that much rain just plastering his windshield, you know it's the end of the picture.'

He drank some more and returned the flask to the glove compartment. Though his jaw was soiled by a beard's sooty beginnings, his fingers and nails were clean. He wiped his lips with the back of his pale hand. Abel supposed that the moment had come: he delivered the bag to Winslow by placing it in the other's lap.

Parting its zipper, Winslow peeped into the bag. 'You want

this soap and Minties and shit?'

'Of course not. I know what's really in there.'

'Doesn't pay to know too much,' Winslow said without vehemence.

Abel opened the door on his side of the car. 'I have to think about getting back to the city.'

'And I need another drink. Take a look around before you go. There's some very nice gardens and crap.'

'Goodbye.'

'Ever been inside, my friend? If you can't stand up for yourself, and I mean *brawl*, you end up with nothing, not even a pair of pants.'

'I don't think I'd care for that.'

Abel got out of the car, shut the door and walked away. After sitting on the train and in the car, he craved exercise. He had left his newspaper in the bag with Winslow, but money and cigarettes were all he needed. The street was lined with the kind of trees one did not see in the city. The ends of their boughs were like knees or the smooth stumps of amputated limbs. Abel thought of the drawings of Vincent van Gogh.

He walked to where the main street of the town became a highway again. Soon he would turn and go back the way he had come, returning to the station and the likelihood of a train, but for the moment he paused on a swath of lawn. He removed his denim jacket and placed it on a municipal picnic table. He rolled up the sleeves of his shirt to give his arms some sun. He wished he had brought a bottle of Coca-Cola. He felt free and unencumbered, sweetened and enriched.

Eighteen

The next day was a Friday. It was late in the morning when I called at the markets. 'Been on the pipe again?' the foreman asked. His Chinese client looked at me with concern.

'I'm chucking it in,' I said.

'I take it you mean the job. The bloke will have your wages from yesterday.'

'There's things I've been meaning to do.'

'He's been sucking the smoke,' the foreman told the Chinese. 'If you ever need a job again, Abel, you know where to come.'

I had rung Omar Kidd the previous evening. He had said we should meet. Now I took a bus to the other end of town and crossed Lambton Quay. The lounge in De Brett's Hotel was spacious and bright. There were vacant tables and chairs in orderly groups. The sight of so much bare carpet was unusual: I was reminded that the bar had just opened.

The odours of beer and disinfectant were stronger at the servery. I asked the elderly barman for a double vodka and orange. 'There's been a good bit of sun,' he said. He spoke with an Irish accent. 'I'm seeing some lovely blooms, I'll give you that in, but we need a spell of rain to be getting the real profusion.'

The table I selected was at some distance from the servery. Over it hung a picture in a frame (whether painting or print, I couldn't tell) depicting a rural scene. A bare-legged farmer stood above a clutch of pumpkins, his socks in podgy rolls about his ankles. I had almost completed the *Dominion* crossword when Kidd arrived. He was carrying his coat.

'I'm running a bit late.'
'You haven't missed a thing.'
'I'll get us some drinks. What's yours?'
He draped his coat on a chair and approached the servery. His shirt was fawn with pinstripes of blue. He moved with a big man's grace, his large chest a cushion to affront. I heard him speak to the barman in deep, cordial tones. When he returned and sat down opposite me, I saw that his collar was grubby.

Kidd sipped his beer and said, 'I'd prefer a coffee.'
'Your shirt needs a wash.'
'I've got an old machine but the hose has perished.'
'You could do the collar in the sink.'
'I suppose I could.' He picked up his coat and reached inside it. 'Here's your money, comrade. I seem to have run out of envelopes.'
'You got a good report from Levin?'
'There are a couple of aspects.'
'Tell me.'
'You shouldn't have gone into the bar. And Winslow says the bag had been tampered with. Keeping you in the dark about the smack – it was for your own protection.'

The four hundred dollars was in notes of ten and twenty. I folded them around my wages from the market. 'A wad.'
'Enough to choke a horse.'
'I suddenly have all this cash. I'm getting rich and I've tossed my job in.' I raised my right buttock from my chair and pushed the slab of money down into the hip pocket of my jeans. 'This pained look you sometimes get, Omar. Am *I* the cause of it?'

'I wish I was blind to my own . . . isolation.' Looking into his beer, Kidd ran his finger around the rim of his glass. 'You're behaving like a clown. You should have hung on to your job. You'll be pissed by two o'clock. I envy you your irresponsibility.'

'People want to stick smack in their veins, that's their business.'

I was looking at Kidd's hand. (I have a theory that what I put on the page is at a subtle remove from my real intentions; that what I commit to paper is in the nature of being an exercise in expedience, an hygienic substitution.) Kidd's hand had come to rest on the table. I saw that the skin on this hand was really a quilt of small, rhomboidal cells. Though large, Kidd would die. And the cells of his skin would suppurate and rot, would sweat and decompose beneath the soil, beneath the steady pressure of the earth.

He raised his eyes to mine. He seemed to steep my face in his gaze. 'You're a criminal,' he said, 'a sociopath like me.'

'Tell me about Vietnam.'

'It could be cold. It rained a lot.'

'I want to know.'

'I went a route. From Da Nang to Quang Tri to Phu Bai. There were places where the hills were green and beautiful.'

'I think of it more as a place where thatched houses were razed, where napalm sucked the limbs off little children.'

'Do you? Is that the case?'

'Did you have to kill anyone?'

'I pulled a man's tooth. I delivered a baby.'

'Heroic.'

'I caused a village to burn. I made old people homeless. And I shot a man. Up close. It was very sudden. It was very abrupt yet very personal. Is this what you want to hear?'

'Someone of your own age?'

'Smaller. Neater. Better. When he was dead, I felt a fondness for him.' Kidd looked down at his glass and raised his eyebrows. 'I'm still there. I hear certain songs on the radio . . . It's as if my life took place in Vietnam.' He rotated his glass a few degrees on the table. There existed between him and alcohol no affinity at all. 'It baffles me why they can't serve coffee in these places.'

'We could go somewhere else.'

Kidd made an effort to smile. 'I've seen enough of you.'
'Thanks.'
'When I get to know you better, I'll tell you about Phu Bai.'
'No need.'
'I wasn't exactly legitimate over there. I'd attached myself to some Yanks. They had necklaces of ears, human ears.'
'It was in the varsity paper.'
'We broke all the rules. We broke *all* the rules. There weren't any rules we didn't break.'
'I think I'm getting your drift.'
'They were burning shit when I arrived, human excrement doused in petrol. When we weren't burning shit we were burning corpses. All in all, in one way or another, there was a lot of smoke. And under the smoke the Saigon River was full of unburned bodies. Chocked. Clogged. No longer navigable. The navy complained. One got used to dead bodies. Because they were dead they were offered every imaginable indignity. "There it is," a grunt might say to you. I watched a soldier kick the brains out of a corpse. "There it is," said the mild lieutenant standing next to me. It's untranslatable. Another common practice was for guys to take Instamatic pictures of their crimes. Bred of all that smoke were pictures of atrocity, a small advance in the art of pornography. There were boys of no previous sexual experience who would shoot the women they'd raped. And all this I got used to.
'Were we really containing Communism? We were serving a great industrial machine and generating huge amounts of wealth in the process. We were consuming things. We were producing minced flesh and corpses for all the big corporations. Dow and Monsanto flourished. It even occurred to me that the world was not meant to know what was going on. Well, in the thick of that welter of savagery, of rapacious addiction to cruelty – how many years since Nazi Germany had been defeated and shamed? – was a stern moral centre. I encountered

it. We had desecrated a cemetery. A monk in saffron robes soaked himself in petrol and set himself on fire before my very eyes.'

'More smoke.'

'He didn't make a sound.'

He looked haggard, bitter, proud. It struck me that Kidd's features did not readily lend themselves to the expression of strong emotions. On his broad face, arousal of any kind seemed to register as fright, as fear, as intense internal discomfort on its way to becoming anger.

His coat contrived to slither peevishly to the floor.

And the day was extending itself: in that bland way in which the mundane is able to make itself less simple, Lincoln Dorne entered the bar.

Nineteen

'What's *this* prick want?'
'Be cool, Omar.'
Dorne came through the nests of vacant chairs. He wore oil-blackened overalls of darkest blue. 'They won't serve me in here,' he said when he reached Abel.
'Omar, this is Link.'
'We'd better not shake,' said Lincoln, showing his soiled hands. 'I was ripped when you rang last night,' he told Abel.
'You seemed to be in *some* sort of difficulty.'
'I'd smoked a few heads. I was having trouble with the language. You ever get that, Omar?'
'No.'
'Man, I was out of it. The simplest sentences – boy.'
The barman was approaching with a cloth. 'The public bar is just next door,' he said. 'A working man in his overalls can feel at ease in there.' He bent to wipe a table, smearing it with lustre.
'We're on our way,' said Abel.
Kidd caught up his coat from the floor. He and Abel stood. The three men filed to the door and out into Lambton Quay. They paused in the shade of the hotel's awning. Invisibly near and loud, a cicada rasped and clicked. Three cars were parked at the kerb, the chrome of their bumpers mirroring the sky. In the sunlight of noon the shadows of things had shrunk, contracted to their tightest shapes. The air was warm and still; in it Abel could smell the oysters and kelp of the harbour's savoury breath.
'Can I drop you anywhere?' Lincoln asked Omar.

'Nowhere. No. But thanks.'

'Mind how you go,' said Abel. He glimpsed in Omar's eyes an onerous advantage, a seniority. Kidd frowned and turned away, toward the courts. His coat seemed to burden his arm. Perhaps the big man's gait was slightly pigeon-toed: the heels of his shoes had been chamfered by wear.

The last of the cars at the kerb was Lincoln's Zephyr. He went to open the door on the driver's side.

'There's somewhere I want to go,' Abel said across the roof. 'Sunday would be a good day. I'll pay you for the petrol if you'll drive me.'

'If we're going any distance in this thing . . .'

'I'd shout you a couple of tyres.'

'You haven't told me where you want to go.'

'My brother knows the details. Perhaps I could ring him from your place.'

Dorne drove them to his flat in Roseneath. When they had reached a street so high that the ocean could be seen in all directions, the car dropped abruptly down a shady drive. Here was a yard of mossy bricks and a garage with a second car in it. The car was up on wooden blocks and covered by a tarpaulin; through the roof of the garage there showed patches of sky and clusters of leaves.

The house was in better repair. Its door stood ajar. Blood followed Dorne inside. The daylight on the other side of the house was visible from the hall. Abel was led to a spacious room with a view of the harbour. The room's elevation seemed to imply tenacity and purchase.

'You rent?' Abel asked.

'Of course.'

A sofa covered by a printed fabric – huge flowers the colours of a parrot's feathers – stood with its back to the view, a telephone beside it on the floor. It was in its emptiness, its underfurnishing, that Lincoln's flat suggested hardship, transience.

'There's some plonk here. You like?'

'I like,' said Abel, and sat down on the sofa. It was positioned away from the window and the sun, away from the heat and silence of noon, in a solitude and silence of its own. Abel dialled Conrad's number. He watched Lincoln pour a sporting measure of the dark wine, a barbecue burgundy from a labelled carafe.

'Why can't you ring at a decent hour?' asked Conrad. His voice came down the line with the force of warmth, of real physical presence.

'Have you talked to Freddie West?'

'You're interrupting something.'

'Electra still?'

'Electra.'

'What have you got that I haven't?' Abel asked.

'Personality? A decent pad? Some pretence of interest in women?'

'Looks is what you've got.'

'And looks.'

'I've been busy. I thought we might go and look at this house of West's.'

'Fair enough,' said Conrad. 'It's at a little place called Rabbit Bay. Freddie gave me directions and a set of keys.'

Lincoln approached the sofa and handed Abel a brimming glass of wine. Abel raised his eyebrows in acknowledgement and thanks.

'Lincoln Dorne will run us up on Sunday,' he told Conrad.

'I don't much want to go. I dislike the country. There's nothing *in* the country. The country leaves a lot to be desired.'

Lincoln had gone from the room when Abel hung up. The tinkle and slosh of someone taking a shower were the only sounds in the house. Abel drank a mouthful of his wine, uncorked too long and now musty and tart. He remembered Kidd, the thing he'd done for Kidd, and was for a moment fearful of detection and justice. Organising a trip to the country was a means of moving away from guilt and dread, of obscuring that earlier excursion.

He finished his wine and crossed to the table. There was nothing for it but to fill his glass again – with more of the lifeless, purple burgundy. Down the hall to his right a door issued steam. Abel felt the need to urinate.

Though a window was ajar, the bathroom was dingy. The ghosts of four pink blooms clouded the window, but the pane was embossed and merely translucent. A string hung from the light switch on the ceiling. The tongue-and-groove of the walls had been painted carelessly: Abel saw a cluster of perfect enamel tears. Dorne stood in the bath beneath a feeble shower. He had not bothered to draw the plastic curtain. The inside of the bath bore livid stains, doleful marks made by the leaking taps. Dorne's buttocks were not much whiter than his thighs. Lincoln the mechanic, Abel thought, whose legs are always covered by overalls. But the legs had shape, a muscular construction, a balanced distribution of strengths. And the hair on Lincoln's arms and legs and chest had been combed by the flow of water down his body. Dorne's trunk seemed younger than his genitals. If somewhat flattened and squared, the penis was big and dark. His broad testicles had suck to the bottom of their pouch.

Abel crossed to the toilet bowl and unzipped. 'That plonk's undrinkable,' he said. 'Let me give you some money.'

'Tyres aren't cheap.'

'What the fuck. I know a guy. Let me give you some money and take you into town.'

Twenty

We went to the Foresters' Arms. Dorne got as drunk and stoned as my money could make him. He won a raw-egg-eating competition and had to go to the toilets to be sick. When he got back he threw a blow at someone and was tapped on the jaw and fell down on his arse – and was ready to start again after a while, resuming his intake of beer with a fresh, improved, more temperate attitude.

The afternoon passed. Soon it was dark outside. Two soldiers from the Salvation Army began to move among the denim jackets and patched jeans of the bar's patrons. They sold copies of *The War Cry*, had coins dropped in their boxes, lingered and were offered lemonade. A man in a beaded headband fired a cap gun at the ceiling. An elderly woman with a basket full of posies moved through the crowd – and some of the drunk and the stoned, the sentimental and the hard of heart, bought bunches of roadside weeds, a dollar a pop.

The back bar was ours, a narrow place like the carriage of a train, well-lit and carpeted and warm, with tables to stand at and tables to sit at, both. At the end of the servery, holding a beer and chewing the fat with the barman, stood Grant Findlay Bruce, otherwise known as Brick, our mischievous guardian angel. I had found him to be tough and mystical, erudite and troubled, irresponsible and chemically savvy – almost anything, in short, one wished him to be. A leather coat too short in the sleeves seemed to bind his dustman's biceps; a youthful face of moderate handsomeness had been puckered and glossed by too many righteous scraps.

We were musicians and painters, would-be musicians and painters, lugubrious actors between demeaning parts, fishermen and window-cleaners, labourers and junkies and prescription-pill addicts. Some of us were nothing very much. One of us would burgle the jukebox to keep himself in cash. But the real criminals tended to drink in the front bar. (One night in there I witnessed a horrible beating, stupefying in its savagery, which no one dared to stop.) Amid the shoulders in faded suede and oilskin, the cloth of a suit might be seen. That Friday night I glimpsed the businessman who carried a silver syringe. And I saw Professor Berquist coming in; he was with a Polish teacher I knew. Though it seemed to have been a long day for Berquist, his cheeks were as pink as ever. He looked fastidious and solvent in his white scarf and Lenin overcoat. The Pole was usually a quarrelsome, sneering downer of glasses of vodka, divinely arrogant. That night he was stiff and mute, holding his head as if he had injured his back. The ice-cream he had bought somewhere was melting all over his fist.

I'd had a couple of vodkas myself. After a few of those it didn't matter that Guy Ace was not around. Working at the market had brought me to a certain level of fitness. And Methedrine had taught me a lesson about my heart, about the sensitivity of its muscular chambers, its nervous ventricles and auricles, to unbidden pharmaceutical stimulation. Nor did pot do for me what I wanted done. Only in dreams of utmost sexual fulfilment was one as winged and invincible, as sublimely free of conscience, as when one had smoked good pot. In its sly, spooky fashion, marijuana was too extreme. It had a knowledge of its own; it was apt to spring surprises; one was grateful when its sprightly company tired. Beer and Valium met a need – when funds were low they surely plugged a gap. But crisp bills bought crisp, spiritous liquors.

For the moment, what I needed was air. I went outside. Dorne's Ford was parked in the alley beside the pub. A dew was forming on the vehicle's bonnet. The car's white panels had attracted a spectral, brassy gloss. I wiped a peephole in the moisture on a window: a man was lying on the back seat, his bearded face toward the amber light. Lincoln had put him there to sleep it off. One of the tyres I had bought that afternoon was serving as his pillow.

Do I make it sound – this life of mine – like an endless party? It was drab and bitter and had to be escaped from. A stimulus repeated is addictive. The life I led was circular and closed, a little bit unreal and onanistic, like real incarceration. I had yet to learn that life is like that anyway, a more or less benign imprisonment in anxiety and doubt. Meanwhile, I was dissatisfied and restless. I knew what it was to think, 'Not here: inspiration is elsewhere; purpose and direction are not to be found in *these* streets, in *this* city.' I was secretly and gravely disappointed by life. This could not be *my* town; this could not be *my* hour or year or century, for *this* was not even my body. Though I put a spring in my step, a little of the grace of sexual momentum, I lacked belief in myself. Those who enjoyed my arms and legs and cock could have no taste, no capacity for aesthetic rigour. I was as keen as a wind: Conrad's was the robustness, the flesh. I struggled in myself with a feeling of contempt for my own talents, but perhaps I could help Conrad to carry himself off, to refine his impersonation of himself. He might finish a few more pictures at Rabbit Bay. If the place was grey and wet, it would match the despondency with which he painted.

I walked to the bottom of dark Egmont St and turned to the west. The abundant light of a Friday night in the city was now ahead of me. Sex with a stranger was what I began to itch for. She might be a small woman, grateful for my prideful bearing, my taciturnity. I wanted her skinny. I wanted her breasts and body to seem new to nakedness; I wanted her nudity to seem to express surprise. Her pubic bush should be broad and disfiguring. Her labia must moisten and distend, seeking to wrap and grip, at the mention of the words 'crotch' or 'bulge' or 'fly'. I wanted her need to be as great as mine, a woman for whom slipping her panties away from her bottom was an act not far in advance of climax. I wanted a woman familiar, from watching it happen, with the pressured, spraying, paroxysmal nature of ejaculation. I wanted a woman in love with male orgasm, its swollen overture and gooey aftermath, a woman who liked to watch the semen fly.

The Seven Seas was a bar on the ground floor of the Hotel St George. There were no plastic palm trees but the ceiling was tinted by lights of red and yellow, bulbs the colours of tropical flowers or fruits. A low wall of stones enclosed a group of saxatile plants, their leaves thick and waxy. And there was a jukebox, its chinks and apertures lit infernally from within.

I bought a drink and took it to a table. The place was not at all busy. I was thinking about the liqueurs ranged behind the bar (an arsenal of bottles multiplied lavishly by mirrors), when –

'Shall I play the jukebox?'

I hadn't seen her coming. She was of medium height, her body sheathed in a black gown. Her forearms and neck were pale. The purple of her lipstick reflected only crudely the far less commonplace violet of her eyes. And her eyes were very watery and bright: they brimmed and sparkled as if she were close to tears, as if she suffered some cruel myopia.

'Can't we just enjoy the quiet?'

'I've seen you about,' she said.

'Have you?'

'I've seen you in the Foresters'.' She put her long-stemmed glass on the table. Her hair was as black as her dress. 'I thought you might be a bit of a prick.'

'Why's that?'

'I don't know, really. Perhaps I thought you looked . . . Never mind.'

'Looked what?'

'Perhaps I thought you looked a bit *head prefect.*'

'You mean athletic, handsome?'
'Not exactly. But fond of yourself, conceited.'
'I'm disappointed.'
'But now I can see you're not. You're quite nice, after all.'
She sat down on the chair closest to mine. Her fingers were innocent of rings, her wrists free of bangles and bracelets. I saw that her thighs were of ideal dimensions. 'Your hair's a bit of a rats' nest,' she told me. 'It could do with a good wash.'
'Possibly. Probably. I've been sleeping a little rough.'
'I'd like to get you upstairs and under a shower. My shampoo's for women but I don't think it would matter.'
'Am I to understand you're in the house?'
'In fact it's lovely hair. Men's hair is so much nicer than women's.'
'I have to confess I've been knocking it about.'
'Knocking your hair about?'
'Knocking myself about. Careless of me, really.'
'You need building up.'
'Yes. Can I get you something to drink?'
But she'd had enough of Chablis and was bored by her surroundings. For her the bar was a set from which the actors had gone, a venue from which the guests had been diverted. Bourbon she wanted, and Coke, and her room on the second floor. We went to the bottlestore and thence into Willis St. The air was cold and dry, the lights in the street blue and crystalline. We walked around the corner into Boulcott St and entered the hotel again through its grand main entrance. I couldn't believe I'd be allowed to pass, that I'd get to the lifts without being challenged. My jeans were worn, my face cheeky, my carriage too libidinous and youthful. As the doors of the lift were closing on the foyer, I took the woman's hand and risked a glance at the reception desk. Not a single face was turned in our direction.

The lift kicked gently into motion. The woman turned to me and flattened her hand against the front of my pants. She was peering up at my face opaquely, her weak eyes like small bodies of oil. 'I'm spending the last of my savings on some comfort,' she told me.

I guessed that her room was not the largest or the most expensive in the hotel. She let us in and I looked for a place to put the bag containing our bottles. I found a kind of desk. To the left of the desk was a window from which could be seen the church of St Mary of the Angels, its porch, steps and balustrade frosted by the glow of the clear night sky.

I turned away from the window. The woman was taking her shoes off. Then she moved across the carpet noiselessly and spread her hands on my chest.

'I'm travelling north. For ages and ages I've worked as an archivist.' She lowered her hands and began to undo my belt. Her knuckles prodded my belly; I heard the slap of unstrapping. 'I'm interested in men. In a library you never look for anything very long. It's either there or it's not.' I was warm and swollen, almost fully erect. 'Perhaps you could pull down your pants. Aren't those delicious words? Just a little further, if you will.' Her fingers were cool and respectful. 'It's just the sort I thought you'd have. I can never understand why they don't leak. Does it hurt when I do that?'

'No. It's good.'

'I'm pushing the blood back down it, right?'

'Correct.'

'And your lovely droopy balls – men are *such* a box of tricks.'

Twenty-one

As he eased himself into her, Abel had a sense of doing the woman a kindness, a favour which was only now beginning, for it was in the nature of this act of charity, this solemn extravagance at the level of skins, of cells and nerves and twinkling mucous membranes, that it should be protracted and episodic.

They coupled on the bed, her back to his stomach. Her nipple was hard and coarse beneath the fingers of his left hand. With his right hand he pushed her belly in, in against her vagina, thus further compressing it around himself.

'Are your getting enough?' he asked.

'My goodness. My word. Mind out.'

'You like a bit of cock?'

'It seems to me . . . I'd certainly have to say . . . Oh heavens, the length of it.'

'You're getting all I've got.'

'It's very good indeed. I'll have to mind my tongue. Just keep that up and . . . *Jesus*.'

She seemed to engage in some brave exertion. He toiled until her climax was over; he guided her over the hill of her distress. And then she seemed to loosen and flood, to bathe his member in warmth as if with the fluid of haemorrhage. He had put her through it; he was responsible and wise. She gulped and breathed and thanked him; she caressed herself down there, at the place where he joined her.

'We're all wet,' she said.

'I'd like you from the front now. I want to see your face. I want to know it's you.'

I want to know it's you.

He disengaged himself. She got out from beneath the shelter of his torso, a thin white animal on the move, still somehow tethered to him. He was kneeling on the bed, presenting his loins to the space where she had been. She turned onto her back but then sat up. And reached for his penis and fingered it gingerly, as if to assure herself of its reality and dimensions, the state of its repair. The urethral opening cupped a drop of dew, semen not yet properly discharged. His blood and energies were banked up tightly yet. He watched her examine him. His organ was at its broadest two finger-widths beneath the umbrella of the flange. It was goose-fleshed and greasy at its base. The surface of most of it was mauve or tan (these hues somewhat latent or occult) with a little of the tautness of scar tissue. The woman appeared to think this column of flesh both congenial and ugly; she seemed to Abel to look at it, inspect it, with a measure of disdain, a fear of what this veined thing could do.

She touched the bead of fluid sitting in the eye of his member. She smeared the clear stuff across his glans. She kissed him lightly on the lips, lay back on the bed and opened her legs to his gaze. Her pubic hair was black, dampened and curled into a suggestion of sparseness. Her labia were gills – or blades or doors. The vulva was designed to be chafed at, to admit the thing that irritated it. Yet hers glistened still. Abel watched her passing her fingers over her clitoris, over her own trigger, that blister shaped like an exclamation mark.

'Do me, honey, angel,' the woman said.

She put her hands to my forearms. I was reminded of the whiteness of her skin, the fineness of her jaw. Her beauty was its own ample standard. The violet eyes were fretful – she had not had enough of me yet – but I also saw in them an emotion I thought of as sisterly, as peculiarly feminine. It had to do with loyalty and deep physical liking. And I wanted to press my chest to her breasts, my stomach to her ribs, my groin and thighs to hers. I wanted our lips and teeth and tongues to meet and to feel her hands on my buttocks and her cheek against my own; I wanted to install myself in her. I wanted to stroke and kiss her tenderly, to bring my feelings to bear: I wanted the folly of that, of that degree of engagement. These were the things I wanted, suddenly – and to spend myself inside her. For to flood and charge with semen the one who inspired this fondness, the one to whom I felt this need to yield, would be the very apex of carnal gratification.

Twenty-two

He lowered his body to hers and placed his narrow hips between her thighs. She trailed her fingers up the length of his penis, traversing all its contours, then grasped it.

She put him to herself with finesse. She moulded herself to him: she pressed and pleasured him with a prodigious licence – and the parts she touched him with were pleasuring themselves.

But he knew he was in trouble. It was clear to him that he would have the utmost difficulty delaying ejaculation. Soon he would brim and spill and their pleasure would be at an end, and what would then remain of this adventure but an awkward absence of friendship? He paused and paused again but it was no good: the derangement of the rhythm of his stroke was itself unhelpful to her, to the woman he wanted to make remember him. And when the accident had happened, when he had made his mess and felt unmanly and maladroit . . . she drew his head to her own and kissed him on the brow.

Abel's flaccid penis remained inside the woman. His mind was in a place of flatness and quiet; she seemed to have joined him in sleeping this non-sleep. At length, beyond the window of the room, the horn of a car sounded. He looked out through his lashes at the woman's lips and nose. 'Nice woman,' he whispered, 'are you with me, strange woman?'

She did not answer. Her eyelids were closed. Abel kissed her on the lips and withdrew from her, unstopping a spring of fluids; she moved quickly to staunch it with a handkerchief. There had barely been enough room on the bed, a single, for two people. Abel had only to roll his body and swing his legs to have his feet on the floor. He crossed to the door and extinguished the light on the ceiling. At once the room was filled to its corners with the misty glow of moon and stars and streetlamps.

'Do you want the curtains?' he asked.

'Could anyone have seen us?'

'Only the man in the moon. Only someone stationed . . .'

'Don't spoil it,' she said. 'I liked the man in the moon.'

Across the ceiling and down one wall of the room, a grid of light propelled itself with slick fidelity to the laws of perspective and projection. Abel lifted the bottle of bourbon from its bag, took the top off it and sniffed at its contents. Bourbon was the softest of spirits, he thought, the sweetest and most popular. He took the bottle over to the bed and placed it on the floor. When he lay back on the bed, the woman rolled her body against his and kissed him on the throat. He felt her breath on his neck and could see and feel her hand on his chest.

'Shall we get into bed?' he asked.

'Why not? Let's pretend we're in a room in the St George.'

'That we met in a bar a half an hour ago.'

'And I brought you to this room to find out what you had.'

He smiled.

'Does that shock you?' she asked.

'Not much.'

'Please don't be shocked. You're too nice to shock. I've seen you about and thought, that guy has yet to be hurt by sex.'

'Have I disappointed you?'

'Oh, sweetheart, don't think that.'

'My name is Abel.'

'There's Ready, Willing – and you, right?'

'Since I don't know it yet, I can't joke about *your* name.'

'Let's imagine my name is Marika Jones.'

'And Marika fancies Abel?'

'But I do, I do. I *love* to be able to see you and touch you, to measure your hard body like this.'

'And do I fancy you?'

'You don't care for me at all. You're a beautiful animal, feral and unthinking.'

'That's not really me. The picture's incomplete.'

'You're a handsome sort of beast. You graze and dream and copulate all day. But evolution is coming, evolution is beginning to work its magic. And one day soon your instincts will begin to worry you.'

'I'm not handsome.'

'You are to me. You are at this moment.'

He drew her to him and she wriggled in beneath him. He covered her with his body. He had a sentimental desire to blanket them both in darkness, to deduct them from the air, the room, from everything. He wanted to sink this woman and himself in a state of utter mindlessness and calm, to make them both impervious to concern of any kind, to the slightest anxiety.

Twenty-three

We parted in the street. She was on her way to a party. I'd had a shower in her room and my hair was still wet. 'I'm going away,' I said. 'I'd like to see you again.'
'You can't have it both ways.'
'No.'
'I'll be at the hotel until the end of next week. Can you remember my name?'
'I think so.'
'So you'll send me a postcard?'
'I might.'
'Don't be upset. Don't get that look. Women run away from that look.'
'Good. Off you pop.'
'Please don't be so cruel. We've done our thing and it's not the end of the world. Now *I'm* sounding dreadful.'
'I like you, Marika.'
'I can see you do, sweetheart. I'm quite sure you do.'
She darkened her violet eyes; she squinted erotically. She touched her palms to my chest and turned away, joining the stream of Friday night shoppers.

And I come *out* of the crowd, depart the past and take a seat in the present. I look up from my pad and my jagged script; I become aware of the place in which I'm writing.

My room has dimmed and shrunk. I put my pad aside and stand. It has rained heavily; it is raining still in an abated and tentative fashion. The dull sky is close. It seems to generate an anti-light, the dimness attending disaster or eclipse. The boards of the fire-escape are bright, the cat's chipped saucer full of rainwater.

At this time yesterday, I went downstairs and through the shop and out into the street. Three doors along is a concern that serves beers and spirits, quiche and expensive salads. There are tables and chairs on low podia. I joined the cook at a table near the window. He is a young man with a shaven head. 'You know what they intend to do?' he asked.

'Remind me.'

'They intend to put a motorway through this whole neighbourhood.'

A waitress brought me coffee. The cup and saucer bore the logo of another, defunct café.

'How did your morning go?' the cook asked me.

'It went.'

'Cooped up in that room. You need a structure, a programme.'

'I went to AA once. A perfectly mad individual talked about how the ancient Egyptians invented colour television.'

'You should write *that* down.'

He looked into the street wistfully. It doesn't occur to him that I know when he is stoned.

'I'm an anarchist, me,' he said a little later.

'Really?'

'I believe in people's ability to order their own affairs.'

'Yes. They like *peace*, for instance. That's a stand-out characteristic.'

'True.'

'They're in love with harmony. And tolerance, of course.'

'Who says they aren't?'

'Not me.'

'You're thinking of Bosnia. You're thinking of the Jews and the cattle trucks.'

'They must have been guilty of *something*.'

'You think so?'

'The flautist and the cobbler. The mason and the ornithologist. It's a principle in police work.'

'What is?'

'That everyone is guilty of something.'

The cook's cellphone began to trill. He picked it up from the table and began to give it all his cautious attention.

THE JADE KNIFE was printed on my cup in a little arch of emerald characters. I remembered writing to Marika Jones from the house at Rabbit Bay. The pen I'd used had been the colour of the letters on my cup. And a sentence I'd used came back to me, as complete as a familiar quotation: 'We want, my prick and I, to stand between you and the world.'

The cook was still busy with his caller. I went to the counter to pay for my coffee. Beside a plate of muffins lay a clipboard; the petition fixed to it had room for my signature. So I put my name between my flimsy neighbourhood and its enemies, those imminent bulldozers.

Twenty-four

The wind was cold and brisk. Against a sky of the very deepest blue, cloud was arranged as if by a gardener's rake. They had left the Zephyr in Pa Road. Abel preceded Lincoln and Electra along a sandy track. To either side of them were lupin and flax.

The stuccoed walls of the shed had been painted a pale lilac. So too the caravan. Abel became aware of the reek of the sea. What the sun had bleached and the salt air corroded, a handyman had covered in bargain-basement colour. Had it been West himself? The caravan was ovoid and cute. It had sunk on perished tyres up to its axles in sand.

Electra was amused by the plaster gnome at the back door of the house. 'Shall we look at the beach,' she asked, 'before we go inside?'

The house faced the sea. Abel led the way along the northern side of it. Sliding glass doors gave onto a patio. To the right were the many flowers, shrubs and trees that hid the house from the road. And through this mass of foliage swung the wind; leaves seethed and flashed their white undersides.

The view from the front of the house was of a blueness, the extensive, wintry sea. The horizon was a blur, an erasure. Where the sand was being blown off the dunes, crisp ridges seemed to rupture and pour.

'Conrad won't like this,' said Electra. 'He hates a cold wind.'

'Summer's on its way,' Abel said. 'What do you reckon, Link?'

'Nice beach. Good house. I liked the look of the town.'

Conrad had decided to stay in Wellington. He had kept to

his bed when Abel called that morning. He hated Sunday drivers, he said, and had caught something and needed a lemon drink. But he had given Abel the keys to the house and instructions as to how to get to it, quoting Freddie West. Could Electra bring him his ganja and cigarette papers? Sigmund the doll would keep him company.

Abel guessed the house to date from the turn of the century. Seen from the front it seemed incongruous, too substantial a structure for the site. And its matt paintwork brought together green, brown and cream – to form an impression in Abel's mind of bucolic muckiness, of fecal camouflage.

He climbed wooden steps to a verandah. The others followed him. He produced the ring of keys Conrad had given him. 'Now for the moment of truth.' But the first key he selected opened the door.

As if his overalls equipped him to do it, Lincoln went ahead down the hall, his hands in his pockets. Abel followed him. The doors of the bedrooms were ajar. Each room revealed a bare wooden floor; each displayed a window's stark prototype. Abel felt that he was being offered boredom and discomfort in colourless doses.

'No beds,' said Lincoln, glancing at Abel.

'Then we'll get some.'

'I saw a place in the village,' said Electra, 'with used fridges and furniture and things.'

Abel looked at her. Blonde coils of hair wound down from under her hat, a lavender woollen hat with a pom-pom. She was wearing a coat of synthetic fur. The sheen of its black fibres seemed stifled and wrong. Her brown eyes shone with liking but how much did they see, how much of him was visible to her? Perhaps he added up to little in her sight. Because she was his brother's, Abel modified and made himself less of a man when he dealt with Electra. She was pervasive and soft; she promised to linger in this house like a scent, like a nebulous blonde light on the retina. Let Conrad deal with her: she was his to animate and direct. Marika Jones was harder, caused more displacement of air. Abel wished Marika were here to confirm and advertise his masculinity.

There was a dead bird in the living room. It had fallen down the chimney and into the fireplace. In this, the largest room of the house, the most depleted and bright, the blackbird seemed to call attention to itself. Lying on its side on the sooty bars of the grate, it constituted a deftness, a neatness, as if supplied or furnished. But it was real enough, Abel saw, and its deadness implied a duration now closed off, an airborne history, a birdy life lived out among the lives of other birds – and to which not a single event could now be added.

Lincoln was standing where a wall had once separated kitchen and living room. Behind him were the glass doors giving onto the patio.

'West seems to have lived in these two rooms,' said Abel. He opened a drawer and found it full of cutlery.

'A poor dead bird,' said Electra. 'Its wee heart has stopped.'

'I'm glad its heart has stopped,' Lincoln said.

'I'm sure you don't mean that.'

'You wouldn't want it flapping around, would you? Frantic to escape and cracking its skull on windows?'

'I'd shoo it though the door.'

The fireplace was made of flat, flinty stones. This stack of silver schist dominated the wall opposite the doors. The long white walls of the room were those of a studio or gallery, but West had left no pictures behind. The glass-topped, wrought-iron table belonged outside on the patio. Abel bent to the grate and lifted the blackbird, bearing its weightlessness on two flat hands. 'I'll bury it,' he said.

'Its little eyes are closed,' said Electra.

Lincoln slid a door open, letting Abel pass onto the patio. The soil at the edge of the garden was sandy and moist. Abel put the bird aside and dug a hole with his hands. Then he placed the bird at the bottom of the hole and pulled the excavated soil forward, covering the bird and filling the hole.

'Done,' Abel said.

'Are you sure it was dead?' asked Lincoln.

'It was stiff and cold, believe me.'

'There are so many birds, even in the city. There should be fallen birds everywhere, but you don't see many.'

'I think I'll get my pack from the car,' said Abel. He felt an urge to wash his hands, to rid them of the taint of the dead bird's living feathers. He looked to the west and the road where the car was parked. The sun had a dark centre.

Twenty-five

Dorne had taken Electra back to Wellington. Abel slept on the floor in a sleeping-bag. That first night in the house, it was as West had said: the sound of waves collapsing onto the beach was profoundly audible. It provided Abel with the soporific notion of a faint phosphorescence.

He rose at eight the next morning. From the kitchen window he could see the mountains to the east. The day was bright and windless. He switched on the Frigidaire and closed its door. While power to the house had not been disconnected, Dorne had had to turn it on at the box. The tap above the sink delivered water in a series of sloppy gouts. Abel's pack yielded coffee, milk and sugar. He boiled water in a saucepan, made coffee and took his steaming cup outside.

It was as if the air had two sides to it, the tepid and the chill. The distant mountains looked hard and precisely made, but in the neighbourhood of the house, a steamy haze lay over the rolling ground and the lupin. Abel opened the door of the caravan. A great many old magazines and paperbacks had been piled up inside. A bicycle had also been left there. Abel dragged it out and upended it, standing it on its saddle and handlebars. It was a sturdy thing, a man's, with a black and glossy frame. When Abel rotated the pedals with his hand, the rear wheel whizzed round.

'Don't jam your fingers.'

Abel looked up from the blur of the bicycle's spokes.

'I'm Evan. I've got some items for you.' The youth wore khaki shorts and his legs were lean and brown.

'I haven't bought anything,' said Abel.

'Mister West rang up and asked me to cart them over.'

'You've got things of West's?'

'He wants you to have them. Beats having them lying around and paying the charges. He's had the items in storage at the depot. When I say items, well, it's a load of old junk, you want my opinion.'

He was holding a pair of coarse leather gloves. Abel guessed him to be about eighteen. His features were fine and dark and of an epicene prettiness. Perhaps he had a little Maori blood.

'Can you get your truck in here?' Abel asked.

'I can back it down the track.'

Soon Evan had the Bedford in position some yards beyond the back of the house. He dropped down from the cab with a gymnast's grace. 'Me mate's off crook,' he said. 'You'll have to give me a hand.'

There were armchairs and dismantled beds. The heaviest thing was a television set.

'You up from the big smoke?'

'I am,' answered Abel.

'It's boring here is all I can say.'

'What do you do with yourself?'

'Work. Bring any dope with you?'

'You ask a lot of questions. Are you some sort of policeman?'

'There's no narks up this way. Last nark we had got frozen to death in the bush. And them cops is *weak*, man. I arm-wrestled one.'

When all the furniture had been taken off the truck – when the pieces of beds had been stacked in the bedrooms and the chairs spread about the living room – Abel made Evan a cup of coffee.

'We get tea at the depot.'

'Ah.'

'There's jobs at the hospital over at Melston.'

'That's good. Tell me something, Evan. Why is Rabbit Bay called Rabbit Bay?'

'Because it looks like a rabbit.'
'Because it looks like a rabbit?'
'Because it's shaped like a rabbit.'
'But it isn't shaped like a rabbit. It's a wide and gentle curve.'
'I know. I was just having you on. But all this bit of coast used to be rabbits, brown as the sand. My dad and his brothers shot them out. Good money, them days, for a single bloke.'

He was being amusing enough as I led him back to his truck. In time he'd dismay and frighten me. There were things his employer trusted him to do, and these he did with suave independence, but I was to learn that Evan was a poignant blend of the callow and the knowing.

Meanwhile, there was the country, the land. I disliked it, of course – and disliked it more than Conrad ever would. It contained something of the forgotten ache of childhood, the fatuous calm of Lyall Bay, the bright, unmoving bitterness of nowhere. It was Lyall Bay without the houses. A dusty suspension misted the air. It was as if a fire burned somewhere, covering the paddocks in a haze, a diffuse blue smoke. The hours before dusk would be silent, would hold and witness nothing but this stillness.

I was (I *am*) afraid. Of emptiness, sterility . . . and waiting. Of the troubling complacency of *things*.

Tuesday came. The afternoon was warm. I left the house and crossed Pa Road, penetrating a cool stand of pines. Emerging from the pines, I began to walk north. Though it couldn't be seen, the sea was to my left. The land was gently undulate and sandy, with a covering of lupin and flax – of flax and flaxen grasses. And there was the DC-3 Freddie had mentioned. It was bigger – no, it was *smaller* than I'd expected. It lay at the edge of a pond with its nose in the water. The aircraft's fuselage was round and intact. Its tail seemed to rest on a mound of vegetation. Because it was lying on its belly, it seemed little taller than a man. The legend on the tail could still be read: LIGHTNING AIR TRANSPORT. The logo featured a bolt of lightning, a zigzag boldly rendered in scarlet. The rest of the aircraft had been grey; now the paint was flaking in handkerchief-sized patches. Where the paint had lifted from the surface of the wing, the metal beneath was milky and dull. I ran my finger along a line of rivets and remembered the plastic models of my childhood, their absolutely static appeal to a boy's imaginings of flight and fiery combat.

The cockpit was inaccessible, the door in the side of the fuselage shut tight. I walked away from the wreck. A feeling of irritation had come over me, and with it a desire to be indoors. I returned to the house and the room I'd chosen to live in. It was at the front of the house and faced the beach; I'd assembled one of West's beds in it. I'd come to a place in which my imagination had room to expand.

I lay on my cot in the fullness of afternoon. As a man may fill a shirt, as a man's activities may fill a room, so my mind could now adjust itself to widened circumstances. I began to think of Marika. We distance ourselves from those in whom we are most deeply interested. But though I excluded her image from the fantasy that attends masturbation, I was not yet in love with Marika, I was not yet in love with her.

On the fourth day, the sky darkened. Abel had placed an armchair just inside the glass doors of the living room. From this he could watch the rain splashing up from the bricks of the patio. A weak and tremulous light seemed to bathe the walls of the room. Late in the morning Abel made a decision. He dug a bottle of sherry from the bottom of his pack. When he had drunk two thirds of the bottle, he made a second decision. (Decision was inevitable and easy. To take another drink or to bomb Hiroshima – both acts proceeded from a common faculty, from the twitching of the same paltry nerve.) He would clear his decks; he would sweep all before him. He would put delay to the sword and write to the Jones girl. An emerald plastic pen came to hand. And paper he had, ah, paper in abundance: he took a stoutish pad from beneath his chair.

21/9/76

Dear Marika,
    I hope this finds you. I'm writing from a place called Rabbit Bay. I was able to take a dip this morning, but now the house is lost in a grey cloud. From where I sit I can see pink hollyhocks, their flowers laden with raindrops.
    I hope I'm drunk enough to make this letter work. Thinking about you and what we did together has made me very fond of you. I see your pin-prick eyes, so dark and hurt-looking.
    My brother is joining me here. He paints, is very nice and has a chick. Why don't you come on up? It's Pa Road near the beach, the only house.
    I think of being inside you and the feel of your nipples against my chest. You are very precious and lovely. There's a little girl in you and she needs protection. We want, my prick and I, to stand between you and the world. I may be a fool who writes drunken letters, not altogether happy ones, but I want you very much I've decided.

                                                    All warmth,
                                                  Abel Blood

Perhaps his letter was merely a scrap of autobiography, something not really meant for Marika's eyes. Those eyes again. He looked at his empty bottle. He wanted another at once. He felt his rapacious will dictate that he get and drink a second bottle of sherry.

Twenty-six

Abel looked for an envelope to put his letter in. Among the items of stationery he kept in a small satchel, he found a doctor's prescription. Some weeks ago he had had toothache: a sympathetic doctor had prescribed Palfium, urging him to go to a dentist as soon as he could afford to. Abel folded the form along its previous creases and slipped it into the pocket of his shirt.

He put on his parka and snapped closed its domes. Getting the bike out of the caravan, Abel was reminded that he had not yet begun his projected work of preparing some ground for the planting of vegetables. He had found a book in the caravan. *The French Lieutenant's Woman* was holding his attention, keeping him from digging and from further exploration of his new environment.

The rain, he thought, had not lessened much. He'd arrive at the township sopping. And it was ages since he'd ridden a bicycle. He mounted. As he circled the space in front of the caravan, the front wheel of the bike slid out from underneath him. He hurt his shin in the fall. For an instant he loathed the alcohol he'd drunk.

He wheeled the bike along the track and remounted it in Pa Road. In minutes he had reached a narrow bridge – and flitted across it. He was leaving the sand and pines of the coast behind: the scenery became more varied and dense, more lush and pastoral. Behind the poplars at the sides of the road, Abel could see the fields of market gardens, long tubes of soil in rain, brown soil and rich.

The sun came out over the township as he got off his bike. A pillar of white air, the dazzling pavement: Abel noticed these things and felt a small delight. He might have pedalled through a vortex of dew, a drenching rainbow. He was wet, nonetheless. He propped the bicycle against the wall of a pub, wiped his face with his hand and flicked water from his fingers.

The bar he entered was empty. From the relative gloom in which he now stood, Abel could see into the public bar next door. He tapped with a coin on the counter in front of him. A barmaid appeared, well-groomed and plump.

'Am I all right in here?' Abel asked.

'That remains to be seen.'

'A sherry, I think. I started the day on sherry.'

'Surprised you can stand.'

'I'm on holiday.'

Though she appeared to disapprove of Abel, the woman poured him a generous measure. 'Fifty cents,' she said.

'Your very good health,' said Abel. He tendered a coin. 'I have to slip up the road. Can I leave my bike outside?'

'Come back in a year, it'll still be there.'

'Nice town.' He smiled. 'Good people.'

'We think so. Can I fill you another drop?'

He left his second drink on the counter. The street outside the hotel was central to the town. Two short rows of buildings faced each other across it. The break in the weather had not been final. Where the sky had healed itself, closing over the sun, a livid pucker had formed. Abel had a sense of having moved closer to the mountains, to the mountainous spine of the island.

The front of the pharmacy was modern and angular. Plates of glass converged. Abel entered the perfumed luxury of the shop. A stealthy man in his thirties came forward. 'What can I do for you, sir?'

'I have a script.'

'May I see it?' The chemist took the prescription. He wore

a smock with a high collar. It was unlike any Abel had seen before.

'It's the molar, I think,' said Abel, 'unless the pain's referred. I've been travelling and that's brought it on.'

'Quite. I see here that this was written six weeks ago.'

'Yes. Could you hurry it up? My wife's in the car.'

'And yours is a Wellington address?'

'We're just down from the zoo. You know the area?'

'I'm wondering if it might not be prudent to see a dentist about this discomfort you're having.'

'Probably. Yes. First thing.'

'Sometimes there develops an untoward tolerance to the pills. I'm fond of saying that tolerance equals addiction.'

'Listening to you is very instructive. Do I look like an addict?'

The chemist grinned. 'Who can say what an addict *looks* like, Mister Flood?'

'Not me, that's for sure. And my name is Blood, with a B.'

One did *not* spot junkies from a hundred paces, no. But Abel knew that they had mannered ways of revealing themselves. It might even be said that they welcomed recognition. If Abel liked to deal in the truth, the world did not allow it. The world wanted something more complex than the truth, more elaborate and baffling.

The cards of pills came in a paper bag. Abel carried the weightless package up the street. He passed a square of lawn and an obelisk. Beyond the lawn was a block of Art Deco toilets. Its windows were syrupy cubes. Above the door of the post office was fixed a mechanical spring with a bulb. Abel bought a single stamp and went to a booth to address his envelope. The booth had sides of corrugated glass.

In the porch at the front of the building, Abel saw the slot he needed. He balanced his letter on the lip of the polished slide – and lifted his fingers. The letter dropped away; he heard it land with a tap inside the box. Almost at once, he began to

99

feel a dread, began to feel that he had done something deeply unlucky. His connection to Marika seemed fragile and redundant, unlikely to bear the weight of his claim on her affections. His infatuation, so recently conceived, was already irksome to him. What he needed now was calm, the steady inner motor an opiate supplies.

Twenty-seven

I finished the glass of sherry I had left in the hotel, but I drank no more that day. When I got back to the house I took ten milligrams of Palfium in a peach-coloured tablet. Four hours later I added a second dose to the first. Long before the second dose kicked in, my fictional toothache had been replaced by the halo of a benign self-regard. My insides were peristaltic and hot, with many productive functions; the thoughts that passed through my brain were remarkable things in themselves. Sitting in my chair by the glass doors, I considered the matter of thoughts as entities, as glowing amoebic trains. That night I walked on the beach, at ease in my own body, at home in the flap of the tepid and saline air. How balanced seemed the stars' distribution, how pure and good the breath in my lungs, feasted on by my blood.

Returning from the beach, I saw a light in the house. Lincoln Dorne stood in the living room. The turntable and speakers of a stereo system were stacked at his feet. 'Look what I scored,' he said as I entered.

'It's good to have you back.'

'Where did the furniture come from?'

I told him. 'Things are coming together for you,' he said. 'What do you do all day?'

'I've been reading.' I picked up the book that was lying beside my chair. '"Yet there rose in him, and inextinguishably, a desire to protect",' I quoted.

'Sounds heavy. A dude gave me this gear. Couldn't pay for some work I'd done on his Chrysler. He threw in a record he hated.'

At the back of the house was a woodpile I had not yet added to. While Lincoln assembled his stereo, I set about laying a fire in the grate. Paper was needed. I went to the caravan for some old newspapers.

The chunks of wood I had piled on the hearth filled the room with a resinous scent. Lincoln complained that his stereo didn't go. I felt a slight relief. 'There's bread and butter,' I said, 'and the pot of stew I made.'

I lit the fire and nurtured it for a while, then I heated the stew and served Lincoln a plate. When he had finished his meal he rolled a joint; allowing him to smoke it on his own, I enjoyed a sense of apartness and freedom from need. He was sitting in an armchair feet from mine. To my left stood a lamp Freddie had sent. Its bulb was at the end of a silver arm, its shade hemispherical and white. In the light of the lamp and the fire, Lincoln and I sat together like veterans of a common enmity or affection.

As he settled into his stone, Lincoln began to thumb his way through a newspaper. 'Electra came to see me,' he said. 'She told me that Conrad was packing up his things, his brushes and paints and all that sort of thing. She thought that they'd be leaving this weekend.'

I was doodling on the pad I kept under my chair. On it I had written, 'A crystal scaffold sinks through the air, not seen so much as known.'

'I think I'll sleep by the fire,' Lincoln said.

'It's just gone eleven.'

'I'll move into a bedroom in the morning.'

'Suit yourself.'

He stood and left the room. A minute later I heard the toilet flush. When Lincoln returned he carried a sleeping-bag. I watched him lay the bag in front of the fire; he opened it out and spread it, forming a blanket or mat.

Lamplight. Firelight.

He began to undress, removing his seaman's jersey and

lowering his jeans. His hips were small and the sides of his buttocks hollow. The V at the front of his underpants was full of an angular mass. When he stepped out of his jeans, the buckle of his belt clunked against the floor. His thighs were long and seemed to consist of a number of slender muscles. The pattern of the hair on his legs in some way qualified the whiteness of the skin.

'I'm stoned,' he said, 'and I want to masturbate.' His eyes were anxious and black.

I felt frightened and repelled. I felt glad and vindicated. 'I've been thinking about a girl,' I said. 'I wrote to her today. If I slept with her again, I think I'd be gone a million.'

'This would be separate. And there's no one here to know.'

His body persuaded me. I was persuaded of nothing. I stood and turned out the lamp and joined him near the fire. I allowed him to lower my fly, to touch me and then to embrace me; I allowed him to draw me down onto the sleeping-bag. His glans seemed to unite qualities of bluntness and sharpness. The flange was conspicuous. I held his testicles while he stimulated himself. He swallowed several times; I could hear the click and pop of his saliva. Before he came he kissed me on the lips. And *when* he came he sprayed himself everywhere; he made stifled sobbing noises, seeming not to want me to hear them. Then he breathed more deeply for a while. There was semen on the inside of my arm and his penis lay across my wrist. I moved my arm and ran my fingers through the hair on his chest.

Twenty-eight

Lincoln repaired his stereo with an inch of wire and a small screwdriver. Over the next two mornings, the music of Neil Young was heard at volume in the house. Young's were skeletal numbers, starved and uncomplicated, cryptic and lapidary. At first Abel listened with something like annoyance. This music was nothing or almost nothing. But it came into being and was remembered: Abel remembered it. A resolute attempt had been made to get as far from meaning as possible, but the dark thump of the bass and the muddled wheeze of the harmonica came to seem familiar, melodic. There was oil and blood in this. Damage had been done: there had been depth and pressure and collapse, and what was left floated.

In the interests of getting rid of it sooner (of simplifying life and resuming the use of alcohol), Abel shared his Palfium with his friend. Lincoln had brought a camera with him. It was, as he explained, 'a cheap Russian copy of the Leica. A very good instrument, if you can get one.' And when the music had stopped, he photographed stillness. Abel watched him work. It was silence that Lincoln wanted his film to register. The surfaces and textures around him, the patterns of light and shade at this feet – he seemed to want to bring these things forward into himself. When he had tired of this intimacy with things, he photographed Abel reading, he photographed Abel digging behind the house. They walked to the DC-3 and Abel stood on a wing and Lincoln snapped him there.

It was Friday afternoon. The sky was overcast, the pond taut and brown. A covey of dragonflies was stalled above the water. Lincoln knocked on the side of the aircraft. He had found a fresh subject for his lens. 'How did it come to be here?' he asked.

'I haven't the slightest idea,' Abel said. Between Lincoln and him, nothing new existed. They were at ease together. A cautious respect for events had always connected them.

Rain began to pit the surface of the pond, large and random drops shaking the brownness. Motion and colour on a tiny scale. And where Lincoln's white shirt was flecked by the drops, his skin began to be visible. The two men set out for the house, Lincoln leading, Abel watching the movements of Lincoln's legs, of the supple buttocks and thighs, the modest exertions of a light physique. And when they gained the house and went inside and stood in the room that Lincoln was occupying –

'I'm thinking about last night,' Abel said.

'We didn't do much.'

'What does it make us, Link?'

'I was randy and whacked. And you look all right.' Lincoln's eyes had dots of sky in them.

'I wanted it as well.'

'Men do these things sometimes . . . and then forget them.' He looked at Abel shyly like a stranger. 'It doesn't change their lives, the way they live their lives. And it doesn't change their feelings toward women.'

'I think of Marika and then I think of you. I think of you inside Marika.'

'You're all worked up about her. There's record levels of hormones washing around your bloodstream. It's a horror scenario at a biochemical level.'

'I don't even know that she'll get my letter. I don't even know that she's interested in me.'

A feeling of expectation troubled Abel. There was no telephone in the house. The best Abel could hope for was a telegram – IMMINENT KISSES MARIKA perhaps. And his Palfium was almost gone: when there should be more there

105

was less. A Friday night at the village was an experiment he had yet to conduct.

Freddie West arrived that evening. He came to the patio in a trim, expensive, clay-coloured coat.

'Trouble in the city?' Abel asked.

'Just let me in. I want to get drunk.' West was holding a bottle of rum.

Abel slid the door closed. 'I was thinking of lighting a fire.'

'And who were you thinking of lighting it under?'

'My guest's just motored off to buy some liquor.'

'I don't suppose I know him. The world's full of people I don't know. The streets are full of blameless strangers.'

'His name's Lincoln Dorne. May I take your coat?'

'And do what with it? You could offer me a glass.'

West rolled his head as if to take a crick out of his neck: the movement was slight and quick, a boxer's mannerism. He stretched out in the armchair opposite Abel's. When Abel switched on the lamp to the right of West's chair, the art-dealer's face was made to look serene, immaculate.

'I seem to recognise this furniture,' he said. 'It dates from the earliest days of my marriage. It belongs to a time when I loved a woman wholeheartedly. One hopes or presumes or merely believes . . . that that special feeling of connection will come again – of its own accord, in time, like a season. But it doesn't, Abel. Not necessarily. One waits and waits – and it doesn't. One ceases to wait, and it doesn't.'

'You must meet a lot of women in your business.'

'I meet them in very artificial circumstances.'

Abel took West's bottle to the bench between living room and kitchen. He took down a tumbler.

'Do I smell grog?' asked Freddie.

'A mixture of rum and water.' Abel returned from the bench and gave West his drink.

'Here's to rum and water. To the vinegar and the sponge,' Freddie said. 'The beginning of the end of the marriage – I suppose it depends on the woman, her range of sexual choices. In Linda's case there were any number of blokes, potential alternatives to me. One night I lost my temper about something. And I saw that that was that, there was absent from her make-up any mechanism for forgetting. She'd never erase the tape, she *couldn't* erase the tape, that particular button had never been installed. Oh, she'd gotten this at her mother's knee all right, this cut-and-run reflex, this trick of never standing still for more.'

'What were you angry about?'

'Her fear of anger, I think. Anyway, the first time in our marriage I raised my voice to register dismay, complaint . . . But that one moment thrived, expunged all the others. For the rest of the time I'd liked her, I'd understood her, I'd believed she meant well. I'd believed she was virtuous, you see, but I hadn't guessed that she couldn't forgive.'

Twenty-nine

Conrad wanted a room with northern light.
'That means Abel's room,' Lincoln said.
'Will you give it to me, brother?'
'I suppose.'
Conrad was in a mood of executive zeal. Sunday had seemed the more likely day for his arrival, but at nine that Saturday morning I'd heard his voice in the kitchen. His present zest might last till lunch-time.
'You could move into the caravan,' said Lincoln.
'I could move bloody anywhere,' I said, 'but I'll take that room at the back.'
Electra was buttering bread. A large pot of saveloys was simmering on the stove. Freddie West was sitting in my chair with a glass of rum and Coca-Cola. 'The weather's turned out nice for you,' he said.
'I need Abel's window,' said Conrad.
'Bob Finch produced his best work in a basement. You couldn't move for empties.'
'You knew him?' Conrad asked.
'I was his first dealer. I thought he was wonderful. I lost him to a mug who ruined both of them.'
'I heard he died of drink.'
'He gassed himself. He died of the smell of gas.'
Lincoln took pictures. We 'lunched'. I shifted my things into a larger room. Wearing yellow kitchen gloves, Electra cleaned the oven. As others moved round him, Freddie kept his seat and continued to drink. At two o'clock he sighed deeply and rose.

'Like summer,' he said as I followed him out of the house. 'The car will be an oven.'

We walked to the red Jaguar he had left in Pa Road the previous night. Conrad's borrowed VW van had a large peace sign on its side. A spectacular clarity extended as far as the mountains. At the side of the road, the leaves of the taupata gleamed. 'I'm enjoying myself,' said West. 'Are you enjoying yourself?'

'Not much.'

Freddie opened the door of the car. Heat wafted out. He lifted a bottle of rum from the driver's seat.

'Bingo.'

'The place isn't mine any more.'

'You must learn to share,' said West. 'Your toys and sweets and women.'

'Can I drive you back to the city when you go?'

'Particularly your women.'

Lincoln and Electra went down to the beach to swim. Conrad began to drink rum with West. They talked of pictures and of painting, and somewhat nervously, as if Conrad's future ability to render anything coherent or beautiful depended on their ignorance of his intentions.

'You don't want – and you shouldn't have – to sweat fucking *blood*, you understand.' West's eyes were closed. 'We're aiming at your first showing. So there'll be a certain discharge in any case – of what I'll call your technical capital.'

'My bag of tricks,' said Conrad.

'Your range of abilities. And don't destroy your drawings.'

'Electra likes to look after them.'

'In what I've seen of your work so far, there are Martian cocks and cunts doing smeary molten things to one another, blue ones and red, am I wrong? I like those very much. But don't get stoned and pissed and ring my home and *never* get drunk and visit the gallery. If Electra agrees that you need it, you can hit me up from time to time for money for materials.'

'Martian?'

Freddie opened his eyes. 'And now I'm going to have that swim I promised myself.'

Lincoln and Electra had returned. West went to the bathroom and changed into black bathing-trunks. I took off my sandals and shirt and followed West to the front door of the house. The wood of the verandah and steps burned my tender soles. A shallow trough in the sand led us toward the beach. To the left were the grey dunes, their shapes crisp and final, timeless desert fixtures today, untouched by any movement of the air.

West's body was more substantial than I'd have guessed. His skin was older than mine; his tan (where had he got it?) had a pink, unhappy tinge. He bore more scars than the average adult: his right elbow had once been made a mess of – and his back was marked by three ivory stars, what might have been the entry wounds of bullets.

He walked into the water. He waded toward the surf. I stripped to my togs by taking off my jeans. The water had lost its chill by the time it had reached my waist. When the first promising wave reached West, he dived into the blue scoop of it, he dived into its glittering concave face. He entered the wave like a spear and disappeared. He entered the wave like a spear or a narrow boat.

A wave is a mouth. A wave ingests, consumes.

Freddie surfaced further out. The sea rose and fell and rose again, allowing me only glimpses of the man. A dynamic medium, this.

'Marvellous in,' he called, his voice diminished by the hiss of surf.

The sea loomed and hid him. When I saw him again he was standing, or seemed to be, and about to launch himself at another wave, a second and bigger hill of imminent water.

The wave washed over Freddie. It continued its advance and broke when it reached me. When it had collapsed and all

I could see was foam – when all I could see were geographies of lather, oceans of beige and continents of froth – pebbles and little shells and gritty sand were being sucked with speed from under my heels. And lost to the greedy undertow was Freddie.

I thought I might fall over. I threw myself forward. My front crawl, I like to think, is a schooled and attractive stroke. It disguises my inability to float. A force impels me, though; something I can never quite believe is a result of my fidelity to principles carries me to where I want to be.

When I paused and trod water, I saw Freddie's back. It was covered by only an inch or two of brine. Lozenges and veins of concentrated light stamped it or trailed across it. His face was in the water and he seemed to be sleeping, sleeping or drinking deep. His hair was a dark mass, robbed of all its blondness and curls. I grasped a handful of hair and pulled his head backwards toward myself. His body rolled into an upright crouch, a foetus in a jar. 'Will you behave?' I yelled.

West's face was upside-down beneath my own. His eyes opened and showed their alarm. Then he straightened in the water as if electrified. My feet touched bottom and as they did the sea sank to my waist. Now Freddie was standing too. He began to gasp and cough and vomit brine.

'You're mad to want to swim!'

'Rum. And saveloys.'

'You shouldn't be in here.'

'If I . . . continue . . . to swim . . . you might have to drain . . . the lake.'

We waded back to the beach. And West was in no mood to linger there; when he had drawn a sufficient number of breaths, I helped him to limp to the house.

Electra was at the sink arranging daffodils. 'Freddie nearly drowned,' I announced.

Conrad had been drinking. Conrad had continued to drink. 'I could fill the world with smoking penises. I could

111

paper these walls with bleeding spacemen's cunts. Couldn't I, Electra?'

'Spacewomen's, Con.'

'Whatever. But I want to return to the modesty of earlier concerns, to the mythological, the pastoral and the green. You don't buy me with a promise of a poncey exhibition.'

'You'll have an exhibition and like it.'

'Poltroon,' said West. 'You might have left me a drink.'

'I think I'll get a dog. The presumption that I'll ever paint again might not be shared by a dog.'

Thirty

To the dark countryside through which it seemed to pour, perhaps the car imparted ease and luxury. Abel was at the wheel of the Jaguar; he felt that he was riding on oil. Prescient and instantaneous, the car's headlights reached forward into the night: what they knew was there, they lit.

'I don't understand the reason for your flight.'

'I want to find a girl,' Abel said.

'Any particular one?' Freddie asked.

'I wrote but then I thought my letter might miss her.'

'You're desperate to feel what you're desperate to feel. There's no helping that. "Love is the delusion that one woman differs from another."'

'What do you know about what I'm feeling?'

'Nothing. Everything. You were strangely abstemious today.'

'I've been on medication.'

'So. You'll be knocking over pharmacies next. What of the future, Abel?'

'I've less of a future now than I had when I left college. I thought the bay might mean something to me. But it's really just as confining and inert as anywhere else I've been. The pills made it seem . . . luckier than it is.'

West took over the driving at Porirua. The return of the car to its owner's control caused Abel a pang of annoyance. During the sweep of the vehicle down Ngauranga Gorge, Abel became aware that he was getting an erection. When the city came into view across the black water, its lights seemed to suggest arousal and expansion, exposure and excitement, various and sharp sexual detonations. Each light represented a sin, a window behind which people touched each other in proscribed and vicious ways. There'd been something odd about Marika's breasts. Each was narrow at the top, Abel recalled; its fullness was in the middle and it tapered toward the nipple. How uniquely feminine those pendulous white bladders had looked, had smelled. Things few others saw were privately revealed, were his to taste and wet with his saliva. The scent of talcum powder; the gentle odour of a woman's armpit; the sour and feral reek of vaginal mucus: these things had been his in a starlit hotel room, and to the worship of them he had brought the length and swollen glans of his firm penis.

What if Marika had left the St George? The city was Abel's home, a known environment. He was skilled at finding people in it. Their trajectories were visible to him; he knew where they would land; he knew where they would settle on any given afternoon. But in Marika's case he was up against a problem: she was a stranger to the city and would behave like one. So she might yet lose him? He thought it unlikely. It would not happen.

West drove slowly through the centre of the city. Couples made their way to the pictures. The Majestic was screening *And Then There Were None*. 'You can drop me at Perrett's Corner,' said Abel.

'It was just as well you were with me in the water.'

'That had occurred to me.'

'Good luck with finding the girl.'

'Thanks.'

'And keep your brother cheeky. Keep him nice and reckless. Reckless and unfinished is the way I want him.'

Abel got out of the car. The gleaming Jaguar pulled away from the kerb with barely a thrum. West neglected to wave. The city was not as warm as Abel had hoped. He was still dressed for the beach – in jeans, a T-shirt and his denim jacket. His capital was dwindling and he had not shaved in a week.

But while he'd been away the city had been swept, cleared of the noise of tired associations.

She was not at the St George. The man behind the desk told Abel this. Marika Jones had quit her room. What the man said he said conclusively, from a standpoint of professional certainty, but with a rueful smile.

'Perhaps she left you with . . .'

'Our guests don't generally . . .'

'Of course not. I must seem naive. Thank you.'

He looked in the Seven Seas. No Marika. He had thought he would know what to do when he failed to find her at the hotel, and in a sense he did. The curt amenities of his friendship with West had given him momentum. Through Saturday night strollers, he walked to the Foresters' Arms. The men in the front bar were wearing suits. The women sat on stools, their legs revealed by the slits in their gowns. Glasses of various shapes crowded the tables. There was cash among the glasses, notes neatly splayed. Impoverished or enriched by the afternoon's events, the bookie was taking a drink with the drunkest of the men, the man with the broadest grin and the loveliest woman. This brittle, moneyed glamour was appealing, but Abel knew its ambiguity.

Fewer people were drinking in the back bar. The jukebox was silent. It was as if the city's reformation, the new and quiet order Abel had imagined he perceived, had slid in off the streets.

Guy Ace stood on his own at a high table. 'Been away somewhere?' he asked. His manner was deferential: where one had been and what one had done were none of his business.

'I've been up north. In body, at least.'

Abel bought a jug of beer and took it to Guy's table. He told Guy about his time away. Guy's hat cast a shadow over the upper half of his face. His beard seemed sparse and noble, a beard in a Rembrandt portrait, with eddies of hair against an amber skin and embryonic spikes at the ends of the moustache. This was a smoky face, mellow and attentive, in which the eyes were brown with lights of blue.

'I've been in Rabbit Bay,' Guy said. 'I had the Norton then and slept on the beach. The girl you mention is working for Zwart.'

'You've lost me.'

'Tony Zwart has opened a place. You can get a meal and a massage. It's a bourbon-in-your-coffee type of deal. I'll walk you over there.'

Abel had been feeling lucky, but now he felt less so. His instincts had proved to be sound: by coming to this bar he had capably located Marika. He presumed that she had spent her savings. But what of the enterprise to which she had then been attracted? Guy helped him finish the beer in the jug and together they left the tavern. In an alley off Manners St, Ace pointed out a neon sign reading RALPH'S.

'His brother's name,' said Guy as they climbed concrete steps. 'Plenty of black paint and some lights on a grid, and you too can be in business. To give him his due, Tony got the floor strengthened and had a pool put in.'

At the top of the stairs was a vestibule and a desk. The front of the desk was upholstered in red leatherette. Abel could smell chlorine.

Mr Zwart was black. He wore a paisley dinner-jacket. Coming out from behind the desk, he shook Guy's hand. 'It's good to see you, Ace.'

'Making a buck?'

'I'm been *down* that road of going for the dollar. Whut I supply now is a *door*. Pipple wunt to pay for comfort and distraction, who am I to impede they desires?'

'This is Abel,' said Guy.

'Say. You crave a nice massage? You like to engage with one of my girls?'

'With *one* of them, yes. The one called Marika.'

'Tell me you not her husband, I'll go and get her quick.'

'Just go and fucking get her.'

'Be nice.' murmured Guy.

The room used by Zwart's staff was commonplace and drab. It might once have been someone's sitting room. An old brown sofa faced a coffee-table; women's coats and bags hung from a wooden tree. A bench and sink had been installed, the plumbing beneath the sink left visible. There were jars of instant coffee and a teapot; an electric jug still steamed tepidly. The room's first-floor window faced Manners St. Abel could look out across an awning at the benches and brick kerbing of Pigeon Park, its lawns yellowed by the glow of streetlamps. The benches and the bricks looked wet, though no rain had fallen.

He heard a door open. He turned away from the window. Marika was wearing an apron like a maid's. 'Hello again,' she said, her tone polite and shy.

'That outfit,' he said.

'A frivolous adornment.'

'Why wear it at all?'

'I think you'd better go.'

'You could have come to me.'

'You're angry and I think you'd better leave.'

He crossed the room and closed the door behind her. Although her lips trembled, she was staying, being brave.

Her mouth was slightly open. And though she appeared in his memory and imagination as a big woman, perhaps as tall as himself, here in front of him in her short white dress and apron, she was reduced at last to proportions truly vulnerable and slight, unmistakably female and feminine. He found her utterly congenial. She looked at him as if deserted by her personality. One of her eyebrows was cocked, but only in feeble reference to her former composure and force, her late ability to captivate and mock. Her familiarity affronted reason; she was known to him in a way he could not understand. He saw a sister in her, a lover and a sister; the shape of her skull and the bones beneath her face spoke to his very marrow.

Her violet eyes were scared and defiant. He admired her

117

for staying put; he admired her for enduring him. Feeling lachrymose and earnest, he put his hand to her face. Her cheeks and her hips were broader than his; he wanted to immerse himself in them.

'What are you doing here?' he asked. 'You're a woman of such striking . . . loveliness.' He tried the word on her: 'loveliness'. No other word would do. 'You've no idea how much I cherish you.' And there was another: 'cherish'.

'I'm glad you've come. I never imagined you would. I didn't think you could really feel that strongly.'

'Look at me. Believe it.'

'I haven't known what to do. I'm not in love with you. I think you shallow and weak, but your letter was very nice. I went and got a carrot. I did it with a carrot.'

'You needn't do it again.'

'You have a memorable anatomy. I think I could like you a lot.'

'You'll like me a lot. I'll make you like me more. You'll like the beach and the sun and having me to fondle.'

'We hope.'

'Look at your lovely knees. You have very pretty knees. I feel a need to protect your knees from harm.'

'You want to do it here?'

'You want to do it too.'

'You're right. I'm wet. I'm falling.'

'Then take your apron off and lift your skirt.'

'Oh, honey, you should shave.'

118

Thirty-one

I was proud of her. She moved me.
And she boarded a train with me the following day; Marika went with me to Rabbit Bay. I carried her only suitcase.
Does the sexual act ever yield its meaning?
A woman I like and respect tells me something she thinks confirms her sophistication. The external evidence persuades me that she leads a life of more than usual sexual mobility. But. In order not to look about the place and see only men she's had sex with, she refuses to sleep with her 'friends'. Her claim may be meant to put me off the scent (off *her* scent, at that), but it takes me in and holds me in thrall, for it has a weird, repellent cogency. This news of the Nineties describes a selfishness, a cynical onanism. It chills me and keeps me awake. I think of another woman, the one in that French film who smokes while she watches a man being tortured. For the moment she is safe from the Nazi torturer. And though her safety is relative and fragile, what she feels, for the moment, is pleasure rather than pain.
The friends of my youth were sexual amateurs. We were democratic and game. The junkies and the homos and the monkeys had not yet come together to cook up Aids.
In the first week of October, I began to work for three hours a day in a local market garden. My fingers and palms became tight and vital-feeling. The embalmed remains of Eva Perón, second wife of the late Juan Perón, were removed from the crypt of the presidential residence and buried in her family's vault in another cemetery in Buenos Aires. Marika bathed and got herself a tan. She would come and stand by my chair,

smelling of a lotion she used, her pubic hair not quite obscured or contained by the wet panel at the front of her bikini.

'You mustn't say you love me,' she said on one occasion. 'A client came to Ralph's while I was there, not the type of man I'd normally look at. He gave me an orgasm.'

'I love and understand you,' I said.

She hung wind-chimes in the window above our bed; she stuck coloured transfers to the pane. Our sheets and our skins were dappled by an ecclesiastic assortment of hues. In bed and on the beach she read *The Magus* or *The New Archive*, two of the four books she had brought with her. And while she read or we made love, cones of incense smouldered in a saucer, becoming perfect cones of the finest ash.

Though Marika tended to keep to our room, she befriended Electra. Sometimes the two women met outside to work in the garden beyond the patio. Electra had weeded and pruned, planting some new bulbs. The northern boundary of the section was marked by pine and macrocarpa. Beneath these stood plum and camellia trees, daffodils and bushes of rosemary. Closer to the patio there flourished primroses and violets, hyacinths and other flowers. Electra had uncovered, at the western end of the garden, a large clay pot in which were growing chives, parsley and dill. Her weeding and pruning had also brought to light a stone lantern and a Buddha made of concrete. Marika shared Electra's pleasure in these finds; the Buddha was youthful and merry.

One morning as I prepared to go to work, two men in suits strayed onto the patio. At first I took them for Mormons.

Thirty-two

'We seem to have run out of road.'
'The road ends at the beach.'
'As we found out. You must be Abel.'
'That's right.'
'I'm Detective Sergeant Harry Keys. This is Detective Constable Brian Bluntcuff.'
'I see.'

Abel did not want the detectives inside the house. With what he hoped would pass for stupidity, he led them through the kitchen and out the back door. The mountains were a jumble of golden and purple planes; the sea's odour was strong; the early sunlight had not yet dispelled the coolness night had brought. Lincoln had taken to sleeping in the caravan. Abel hoped he would not emerge to complicate matters.

Harry Keys was younger than his partner. His blue eyes and longish hair suggested the athlete. The moustache was blond and lank. He took Abel's forearms in his hands and turned them toward himself. His touch was as gentle as a good dentist's.

'No evidence on these . . . of any misbehaviour.' He dropped Abel's arms and moved back a pace. 'You've been missing from your usual haunts, Abel. You haven't been seen in the Foresters' so much.'

'I was in the Foresters' two Saturdays back.'
'Were you? Were you really? Who did you see there?'
'It looked as if the Preston boys had just blown a tank.'
'They'd just sold a horse. Who did you talk to?'
'I talked to Guy Ace.'

'Now there's a name to conjure with. We had occasion to look through his garage the other day. Certain substances have been coming through the port.'

Abel said nothing.

'Do you know this man at all?'

Keys handed Abel a photograph. It was a coloured head-and-shoulders of Omar Kidd in the street. He had not noticed the camera. This was Kidd in another incarnation; he was represented as being radically younger or older than when Abel had last seen him. It was as if his eyebrows and eyelashes had been darkened by some process, his cheeks electively tightened in a clinic. Perhaps he was wearing make-up or a toupee, had been lying on a Mediterranean beach. Though apparently in motion, Kidd looked sybaritic and idle.

'It's not a very good likeness,' said Abel.

'No?'

'It looks like a frame from a silent movie.'

'We had to work from an old print. We aged him and cut his hair.'

'The man's an acquaintance, nothing more. A rather sad and broken ex-soldier. Aimless, worried, sinking.'

'Sinking?'

'Drifting into mediocrity.'

'And you formed these impressions . . . on the strength of what?'

'A meeting in a bar.'

'A meeting in a bar? Just the one?'

'We only met the once, yes.'

'He didn't want it up the bum? He didn't offer you money?'

'He didn't offer me money. And I never saw him again.'

'Do we believe him, Brian?'

At Keys' back, the other detective shrugged. Who was he to read degrees of mendacity, perversity, perversion?

'People talk,' said Keys in a smaller voice. 'Kidd's name keeps coming up. You don't have his address, by any chance?'

'No,' Abel said.

Keys turned to Bluntcuff, who had folded his arms. 'Let's go through it, Brian. Abel here has moved up from Wellington and now occupies a house he doesn't own. He has a number of guests, all unemployed, and about whom, for the time being, the less said the better. The question is, what was he doing on the seventeenth of last month?' He turned to face Abel again. 'What were you doing, Abel?'

The carriage entered a tunnel. There was violence in the event, the gust of collision avoided.

The warmth of expectation had narrowed Keys' pale eyes. His chin had a cleft his razor failed to sound. Bluntcuff was watching with a sort of nervous boredom, as if Abel were a witness badly in need of prompting. But it had come, as Abel had known it would, a question about the day he had taken the train to Levin.

'Beats me. I've no idea. Whole months go by,' said Abel, 'and I never know the date.'

The man he'd met in Levin – what had he said about gaol? 'If you can't stand up for yourself, and I mean brawl, you end up with nothing, not even a pair of pants.' The scent of the dew and the stink of the sea were things to be defended and held to. Abel lifted a shovel away from the side of the caravan. Its shaft felt cool and smooth. The caravan's window was a mess of streaming wetness; the low sun struck the window and was orangely deflected. A huge, furry bee descended past Abel's face.

'The seventeenth was a Friday,' said Keys. 'Does that help you remember?'

It had *not* been on a Friday that Abel had travelled. 'Pick any date,' he said, 'and ask me where I was and what I did. I've no memory for that sort of thing.'

'We're filling a box with things,' said Keys, 'with pieces of information. Sooner or later the items in the box . . .'

'. . . reach a critical mass,' said Bluntcuff.

123

No. Friday had *followed* his trip to Levin. On *Friday* Kidd had paid him and talked about . . .

'I have to go to work. I don't know anything about whatever it is that's coming off the wharves.'

'Smack,' said Keys.

'And acid,' added Bluntcuff. He sighed. 'You've got a very good soil here. Any retired person could do wonders with this soil.'

Thirty-three

To the north was a river. On the southern bank of the river was a hut. This had become known to the locals as Drunk John's Shack. The end of Lightning Air Transport had come with the landing of its aeroplane in a field not far from Freddie West's house. (The house was not yet West's; the aircraft was the company's sole remaining asset.) The pilot of the DC-3 had limped away from the site of his final touchdown. Returning from the township that night, he had lit a fire on the river-bank and drunk the best part of a bottle of whisky. Time had brought the decade to a close, but not before allowing there to rise, to organise itself near the river, John's imperfect bower of stones and timbers.

The historian was Mr Yee, Abel's employer. He had been a little boy when the DC-3 had come, had suddenly shown its belly above his father's barn. Its port propeller had been starkly inert; the engine behind that had squirted smoke, an opulent blue smoke like an ink.

At noon on the Friday of the detectives' visit, Abel cycled home from work. He found Marika lying on their bed. She wore big-lensed spectacles when reading. Having made a pot of tea and taken it to the bedroom, Abel told Marika Mr Yee's story.

'That's nice,' she said, putting her book aside. 'What did those policemen want this morning?'

'I told you.'

'Not properly.'

'I don't think they knew, themselves.'

'I didn't know you were a criminal.'

'Supposing I was, would it make me sexier?'
'Not very. I like my men to be honest and gentle.'
'You don't believe in gentle criminals?'
'Of course not. Someone always gets coshed or whatever they call it.'
'Are you studying for some sort of exam?'
'What do you mean?'
'*The New Archive*. Are you leaving me and going back to work?'
'I'll have to soon, I suppose. Find some kind of work, I mean.'
'There's something you can do for me right now.'

That afternoon they walked to the river. Morning had brought flashes of reddish light. The sun had seemed to dart from place to place, but it had since been extinguished. The sky was now its own geography, a primitive landscape of volcanic character, a waste of mud and ashes. Only far out to sea did the cloud seem to end – in another, subtly brighter stripe of greyness. From the porch of Drunk John's Shack there was a view of a mass of silver stones, a shelf of laundered rubble. On a lower level still was the stream, as dull as the sea from which it seemed to ebb, though its surface glittered whitely in places. Its northern bank was a wall of mustard-coloured rock, low and topped by scrub.

It was warm here, and quiet. The quiet was really a pleasant set of sounds. It consisted of the muted hiss of surf and the pebbly, sluicing noise of the river. The livid horns and fissures of the cloud

Marika held my hand. 'This pilot of yours,' she said. 'Men seem to have a sneaking respect for chaps who drink themselves to death.'

'One doesn't really drink oneself to death.'
'I knew you wouldn't think so.'
'I'll tell you what happens. You slow yourself down and fate catches up. You're overtaken by accidents and illness.'

'In other words, it's all a bit unfair.'
'The man who built this hut. If he couldn't be a pilot anymore . . .'
'. . . he'd stay put and sulk?'
'And then the delirium tremens crashing about on the roof.'
She laughed at that and dropped Abel's hand. How simple she could be, how simply herself. Her amusement lit her congested, violet eyes. 'I notice you're not drinking very much.'
'You don't notice properly,' he said. 'I'm not drinking at all.'
'Are you in training for something?'
'I'm in the middle of the main event. I've got a little friction sore to prove . . .'
'Don't show it to me here. We're on an outing. I've even brought some lunch.'

The hut stood at the top of a rise, its back to a lush bank, its walls pressed in upon by bushes of flax. Its design combined the stout and the slender. The lower half was of stones, lavishly cemented. From these there rose a wooden superstructure. Into the stones and planks were set a door and a somewhat broader window, the latter not quite square. The corrugated iron roof sloped backward. At the front of the hut, the roof formed a porch. This was supported by four-by-two uprights, pillars silvered by the elements. The floor of the porch consisted of pink flagstones. The architect of this modest folly had touched it with his bibulous élan; the hut succeeded in looking trapezoid and jaunty, not altogether permanent or safe.

The door of the hut had no handle or lock. It opened inward freely to reveal a cement floor, a dustless glow, an unremarkable nothing. Abel stepped inside. His head touched the ceiling, the roof. He had the feeling of being in the basement of a house. A wintry peace seemed to fog the only window.

'You're not getting me in there,' called Marika.

Abel left the hut and closed the door. A bench like a pew stood at the front of the hut. Marika had brought a paper bag with her: she put it down on the bench. 'Are you hungry?' she asked.

'Not very.'

'All right, then – are you happy?'

'Not completely.'

'Why not?'

'I'm scared of what I'll feel when you leave.'

'That's not for ages yet.'

'You've been thinking about it?'

'No. A little bit.'

'Where will you go?'

'Australia, perhaps. Flinders looks promising.'

'I find it hard to believe . . . that I'll ever feel differently about you, that I'll ever not mind what you do.'

They stood face to face. He saw that she was frightened or embarrassed. She put her arms round his neck.

Abel tried again. 'Up here alone, before I wrote, I felt very lonely. You were on your own somewhere, distressed and penniless. I wanted to rescue you. I wanted to be the end of your search.'

'God help us both,' she said, pressing her face to his chest.

'Listen. Marika. I *chose* you.'

She tightened her grip on him; she hugged him to herself: this taller person was absurdly distant, remote from common sense and common knowledge.

'We never really love,' Marika said. 'What we love in others is really a reflection. What we love in others is the image of ourselves.'

The visceral and brotherly in me had been dealt a stinging rebuke. I'd been repulsed and silenced. Marika lifted her head away from my shirt. Far from being tearful, her violet eyes were dry. She could not bring herself to smile, to qualify her sudden cruelty. Yet her eyes seemed milder, clearer, more discernibly wilful. She had found a cure for her conjunctivitis – in salty air and the cawing of gulls, in a pretence of sexual independence. She was trying not to think about the future: it would include a house and a car, and a new, improved, less sensitive boyfriend, one with a browner skin and a bigger penis. Her features were smooth and defiant, had been fashioned with confidence, had been remade brightly. Her face was firm and good, astonishingly dear; of all the flesh in the world, hers was the most precious. Why were all the men who'd ever used her not here to compete for her? What was wrong with them, that they had not wanted more and more of her?

Carnivorous seagulls. Their vocal truculence. Birds belonging in fenced rubbish tips. White-winged and muscular, they wheeled and roistered through the murky air.

I took her head in my arms; I buried my nose in her hair. 'You're it, you know. You're all I ever wanted.'

'I'm not a Christmas present,' she said.

Thirty-four

When did it take hold in the world, this fear of emotional attachment?

With our expertise – with our psychology – we can have sex as it's never been had before; we can be free of sex but have it always on tap. Yes, we can *store* it, sex-enhanced sex. In bars and nightclubs lit like sexual laboratories, the ambience is free of the musk of sentiment. The sexual zone as insulated and sealed: when was it constructed? For today sex is accessed with a swipe card, it opens to the sound of a patron's voice.

And there are yet more cards. Money and cards, Gold Cards: they buy caresses, they buy touching and pleasure. We need never soil our hands or trouble our hearts. This fashion for the avoidance of the real (this pampered taste for painless, bloodless sex) bespeaks an acceptance of substitution and surrogacy. The current wisdom whispers 'She'll be gone before morning' or 'You need never see him again.' Though the top of his ear enchant and soften you, though the line of her buttock and thigh bring you to your knees, *they are not worth the pain of engagement*. Pretend she's another; imagine he's someone else. The luxury bought by this way of doing things is that of remembering how powerfully total sex once was, while remaining uncommitted and inert.

I never play. I'm never involved. The grim and disappointed – those starved of life by life – they don't have a card, you see, their voices have the wrong timbre and won't do the trick.

All this causes me sorrow. And gives me an appetite for pornography, for pictures. What I really want to look at I have to be brave to buy. 'Will that be all, sir?' Does the man mean this transaction is legal? (Nowadays, it is actually the homosexuals among us who *least* believe in the possibilities of promiscuity.) To take my mind off sex – off my own bitter sexual isolation – I set myself tasks. One day, for instance, I will go to the top of the vast and tall new building we have here in the city. It is big and it has come to earth. I think it colossal; *it* thinks it's colossal. It is flash and absurd and titanic; look to the top of it and your eyes water. Get inside and ah, it is empty; it contains so much air that it has its own climate. Marble, brass, ceramics; wide pools and ponds of swirling limpid water: one mounts through tiers of these on a steep escalator. In a thousand years' time, this cavern will contain a rain forest, an Amazon. Abroad in some Athens of the hereafter, Drunk John may have conceived this commodious citadel, this ingenuous immensity, chalking it out in the middle of a square.

And of my own immediate neighbourhood? It's of balsawood; it'll soon be crushed and flattened, as things of balsa and cardboard are. Under a pluvial sky, the cat will go its way and I'll go mine; the nostalgic bone-carvers and hairdressers will find cheap premises elsewhere. The cook (you have met the cook) – the cook was converted to Christianity, was reborn, was saved, but is doing time for bottling a bloke. *I* don't go around bottling or braining blokes. There's something I *do* do though. In an altogether different spirit from that in which, if allowed, I might ride to the top of a very tall building, I drink a little. From time to time, I drink. For an hour or two I'm ablaze with pride and youthful confidence. I'm young again and brisk and sharp and pretty; I like myself once more. It is hardly to be believed that my life is over: I enjoy or endure the blissful delusion that *there will be more*. I flare, I fume – for an hour I'm incandescent. But I consume myself. I stay away from you and you and you; I keep to this room and talk to myself until . . . my speech is slurred and I can't stand fucking upright. And even as I'm doing these things to myself, I pity myself the return I shall have to make to the dead brain and body of my shameful sobriety.

I've been known to scratch at these pages while imbibing. A half a bottle of sherry evaporates and my writing becomes astonishing, baroque. I'm drinking tea again. We need a symbol here, an asterisk or star. What's needed is a dolphin or a shell, a little something to signal my return to my adolescent subject, my distant story. Soon Christmas would come to Rabbit Bay, a fact which may or may not have occurred to Marika when we last heard from her. There were often days of continuous sunshine. Sunflowers swayed above the garden; Lincoln parked a frowning Citröen beside the garage; dole cheques began to arrive for Electra. She took to hiring a horse called Buttons from a farmlet near the village.

What happens next is Evan. Evan happens next.

Thirty-five

There was a cinema in the township. Its facade was modest, compact, four narrow glass doors beneath a strip of hoarding. A portable board like a headstone stood on the pavement outside the theatre. It was of mahogany and bore the theatre's name and session times in slightly tarnished gilt. Though the Strand was miles from the sea, a sifting of familiar grey sand lay in the gutter beneath the mahogany board. Heat and light and sand: Abel speculated that into the dark church of the theatre's auditorium, these things leaked companionably.

A door in the Strand's foyer connected the theatre with the milk bar in the next building. In the tiled white coolness of this latter, Marika had been given a part-time job. She worked in the afternoons, from Thursday to Saturday. Under the shaped and chunky cardboard illustrations of froth-capped milkshakes and sundaes in glass dishes, Marika faced her public. There was a machine, a small heated vat, in which she had learned to dip ice-creams, coating them in thin veneers of fast-drying chocolate.

It was the first Thursday in December. The main street of the village seemed bent and foreshortened by the heat of afternoon. There were no customers in the milk bar and Marika was alone behind the counter. She was wearing a short white coat.

'You look like a doctor,' said Abel.
'I'm handling food.'
'A vanilla, please, if you're not too busy.'
'Have you been watching the picture?'
'I'm not in the mood for a *Carry On* anything.'

'I hear them laughing like drains.'

Marika held a scoop. She reached with it into a refrigerated tub. The air down there was frosty, visible. Abel thought of liquid oxygen.

'One lump or two?' asked Marika.

'Just the one will do.' Abel looked at the empty booths behind him, then out the big front window and into the street. 'You see that kid across the road? He brought the furniture to the house.'

'I can't look just now.'

'Evan's his name. He's odd.'

Marika handed Abel his ice-cream. The lid of the tub made a rubbery thump as she replaced it. 'Now I can look,' she said.

'Just over there.'

'The one in the shorts?'

'That's him.'

'I think he's lovely.'

They watched him cross the street. His eyes were on the theatre next door. If his face was androgynous, his legs were masculine. He walked with the unhurried confidence of someone who was always in motion, always ready to apply his know-how, his strength. His black-eyed gaze evinced curiosity and innocence, a boyish readiness to enlist and partake. When he reached the kerb he looked inside the milk bar (for girlfriends, for cigarette-smoking mates?) and saw Abel's smile of recognition.

'Hello again,' said Abel when Evan stood before him. 'What's amusing you?'

'You're eating an ice-cream.'

'So I am. Wellingtonians are very big on ice-creams.'

'That's true,' said Marika.

Evan took her in.

'I'm surprised you don't know Marika,' Abel said. 'She's with me out at the house.'

'I'm very pleased to meet you,' Evan said.
'Any friend of Abel's,' said Marika.
'Settling in all right?' Evan asked Abel.
'Yes.'
'On the phone at all?'
'Not yet.'
'Running into you reminds me. Could we have a private word?'

They moved to a booth and sat down facing each other. A small crowd of people drifted into the milk bar, Maori women in pairs and elderly married couples; Abel deduced that it was intermission time at the Strand. 'What's on your mind?' he asked.

'I've seen you coming and going,' said Evan. 'I've seen you partying and the Jag parked in the road.'

'So?'

'I take the truck to Melston once a week. There's a room in the hospital.'

'Go on.'

'I can get you morphine and plenty of it. They give me a key.'

'More fool them.'

'One day a week, I have this key for an hour.'

'And what would I do with morphine?'

'Entirely up to you.'

'You can say that again. It *would* be up to me. Look here, Evan my friend, even our talking this way constitutes conspiracy, they have little gadgets like buttons, they could be listening at this very moment, they have little microphones like peas.'

'You're chicken.'

'Fucking right I'm chicken. And I want you to forget all about rooms in hospitals and morphine and me. There's no connection between morphine and me. Got it?'

'Keep your hair on.'

'You think I'm being unfriendly? I'm not being unfriendly.'
Chimes signalled the end of the Strand's intermission.

'Your ice-cream's dripping,' Evan said morosely. 'And what would they be doing bugging you?'

Thirty-six

Sunday afternoon was cloudless and warm. The windows in Conrad's room had been lifted as high as their sashes would allow.

In order to obtain continuity of palette, Conrad had worked simultaneously on his two new canvases. These pictures were devoid of any description of nature, of all anatomical allusion. The shapes they framed were those one might glimpse through a door, a crack. There were surprises, too, in Conrad's use of colour: the usual blacks and reds were there, his staples, but then came that fleshy cream he'd invented and which Abel associated with a specific childhood confection. Conrad had also employed avian pinks and greys which seemed to sweat, to humidify his work. In later years, Abel was to wonder if his brother's abstract essays had not set a fashion in office colour schemes.

'You can smell them,' Abel said. 'They're about to rain, to thunder.'

'You don't miss my dwarfs? The broken noses and lolling tongues?'

'Is that what they were?'

'My starships and plastic masks?'

'Not a bit.'

'Good. These are the paintings of my maturity.'

'You don't say.'

'I do bloody say. Electra? Haven't I been saying that these . . .'

'That's *exactly* what you've been saying. But you're only twenty-three, Con. And you drew *so* beautifully.'

'There's draughtsmanship in these. Look at the tensions. They're snapshots of erotic cataclysm.'

'I miss the human element,' said Lincoln.

Leaning against the walls and hiding the skirting-board, Conrad's pictures were ranged around his room. He had brought them to Rabbit Bay in the van that remained parked in Pa Road. The odours of linseed oil and turpentine reminded Abel of his Uncle Athol and his pathetic hobby. This talent for enjoying viscosity and bristles had come down to Conrad in chessboard, leap-frog fashion. Abel was standing very close to Conrad. And his brother's unshaven gauntness and tousled head had for Abel their very own aroma, that of the bedroom and damp napkins, of the breathing, bubbling closeness of childhood. In moments like this, constructed of aspiration and qualified success, Abel could smell on Conrad's breath infancy's milk and infancy's tragedies.

Electra ran her hand down Conrad's back. 'What's this about cataclysms?' she asked.

'Don't I shake and scorch you?'

Conrad continued to look at the second of his new paintings; he had not yet taken it off the easel. Abel left his side and went to stand by the door. Marika sat down on the unmade bed and picked up Sigmund the doll. 'I think Conrad's very lucky,' she said. 'He's keeping himself so busy he doesn't notice the tedious dullness here.'

Electra's frown assented. She readily accepted what was true and obvious.

'I was reluctant to come,' said Conrad, 'but I find it's perfect if I don't go outside.'

'I don't know what we'd do without my dole money,' said Electra.

'You can have my job at the milk bar.'

'The trouble is,' said Lincoln, 'we don't go to the pub and we don't know any locals.'

'I meet them,' said Marika. 'They're very inquisitive.'

'There's booze in the kitchen no one touches,' said Lincoln. His jeans were patched and faded, his shirt unbuttoned. 'I've brought home vodka and whisky but no one drinks them.'

'What are your thoughts, Abel?' Electra asked.

'Everyone's got to be somewhere. I ride my bike to work. I pull my cabbages. The loveliest woman in the universe has come to live with me.'

Electra lay back on the bed beside Marika. Beneath her thin summer dress, her pubic bone was prominent. The puffed-up curls of her blonde hair lay near the other's thigh. Electra and Marika: the dark-skinned English rose and the fair-skinned Gypsy. Electra placed her hand on her groin (the act was innocent of any apparent intention) and Abel became aware of the mass of his genitals, no longer quite inert. He allowed himself a moment's belief – in a fantasy of rigorous nakedness, of sweating female stomachs.

'I miss my music,' said Electra, looking at the ceiling. 'It's nice to exercise Buttons, but he's not a well horse.'

'I said I'd mop the milk bar,' said Marika.

'There's peas and pumpkin and spuds,' said Electra, 'and that nice leg of lamb. If we didn't sit down to it till eightish . . .'

Lincoln's Zephyr was off the road and his Citröen was not yet going. He borrowed the keys to the van and offered to drive Marika into the village. She hinted that she would like Abel's company. At the end of Pa Road, Lincoln turned the van with energetic movements of his wrists. The pines were at their tallest here. They seemed to afford a hushed shelter, a charmed shade; one could look into the depths of them and see a sunny green air like the water in an aquarium. On the drive into town, Abel saw the place where he worked, its grey, familiar acres of furrowed soil. Out in the most northerly corner of the property, beneath the blue stipple of a line of distant poplars, Mr Yee's tractor was evident, a tiny and unmoving yellow speck. The meaty underside of Abel's forearm rested on the hot panel of the van's door. Nearer the township were houses whose gardens seemed to brim with foliage-covered boughs. Abel saw verandahs which were themselves gardens: thicknesses of leaves and mauve and orange flowers clothed posts and rafters. Into the petrol-scented air of the van's cab, the fragrance of honeysuckle was draughted.

Pa Road ended. Lincoln turned the van into the main street of the township. He stopped outside the Strand. 'I'll get some vinegar,' he said. 'She'll need some if she's doing mint sauce.'

'We won't want picking up,' said Marika. 'We'll walk back when I've finished here.'

Abel got down from the van. Marika followed him. She was wearing jeans and a blouse she had knotted over her midriff. Abel shut the door of the van and the vehicle moved off. Looking up the street, Abel felt the need for sunglasses; at only a little distance, the road seemed to liquefy and tremble.

There was no one about. Marika had a key to the milk bar. Abel thought that those whose business was with locks and security, with the regulation of access to goods and premises, were insufficiently stringent. All this laxness with keys was his to exploit, but he had no intention of exploiting anyone or anything. Not today. Not tomorrow.

He slipped into the shop and sat down in one of the booths. Marika shut the door and went behind the counter. 'There's a couple of shelves that need restocking. I'll just do a quick mop and then I'll show you the theatre.'

He could see her clothes through the clear plastic apron she was putting on. He could still see her navel. He smiled. 'You think Lincoln's attractive?'

'A lot of men are.'

'But Lincoln?'

'He's boyish and sturdy. Now those are not qualities I'd normally rave about, but with his shirt open and those chocolate-coloured nipples . . .' She feigned a shiver beginning at her hips.

'Do you think he'd have a big one?'

'Enormous, I should think. Disproportionate, like a baby's.'

The whiteness of tiles. A coolness in which could be heard the tinkling percolations of the big refrigerator. Abel lit a cigarette. Marika filled a bucket at the sink behind the counter. From a yellow bottle, she added a squirt of detergent to the hot water. The scent of lemons reached Abel. A braid of shivering smoke ascended from the tip of his cigarette. Marika worked with no conspicuous vigour or speed, but within ten minutes she had mopped the floor behind and in front of the counter.

'You came all this way to do that?'

'It got us out of the house.'

Marika emptied her bucket and took her apron off. Then, running her palms down her denim-clad thighs, she came out from behind the counter. 'Time for the tour,' she said. 'You'd better put your smoke out.'

A sliding panel of enamelled hardboard gave into the foyer of the Strand. Light from the street was admitted through the theatre's glass doors. The emptiness of the place brought home to Abel the originality of the decor. Its carpet was brick-red and its walls olive-green. Over the ticket office was a shelf on which was perched a grotesque in the form of a merman. The statuette's body was that of a fish; its head was the likeness of an ancient Egyptian king, with striped head-dress, a golden face and black-pupilled eyes. At the foot of a flight of stairs, a board was fixed to the wall. DRESS CIRCLE said the letters on the board; the gloved hand pointing upwards had also been rendered in gilt. Mounted on the newel at the bottom of the stairs was the representation of a flower, plates of frosted glass in a framework of lead. It would be lit from within when the theatre was in use.

Marika threw a plain domestic switch and light fell on the stairs. 'Shall we go up?' she asked.

Above the stairs were pairs of shaded bulbs linked by plaster lanyards. On the landing at the top of the stairs, a kind of easel stood. To the baize-covered board on the easel was pinned an advertisement written with a felt-tipped pen. 'One Screening Only – Sunday 12th at 8pm – Bernardo Bertolucci's *The Conformist* with Jean-Louis Trintignant.' Abel had seen this movie three times. He could not have said why he passed the poster in silence, not bothering to draw Marika's attention to it.

He followed Marika onto the upper tier of the auditorium. The view from the back of the banked rows of seats was one of dilute gloom. To the left and right of the proscenium arch were emergency-exit doors. The word EXIT burned redly over the door to Abel's right, but the other door was standing open, apparently hooked back, so that the glare of the afternoon outside seemed to bulge into the theatre. In the glow from the open door – in the wash of a light at a distance from its source – the left-hand column of the proscenium was visible in relief. Abel saw a masculine figure, that of a youthful faun perhaps, whose naked and flat-bellied trunk descended into the crumpled drapery of a girdle, the whole statue having a lustreless, bronzed appearance.

Abel felt Marika take his hand. And almost at once his ankle felt a friction, the brushing pressure of a moving thing. 'A bloody *cat*,' he said.

'They've shut up the downstairs. Fred lurks around up here now, don't you, Fred?'

'Can I look in the room where the projectors live?'

'The projectionist has got the only key.'

They made their way gingerly down an aisle. Abel's feet kept coming up against the cat. It occurred to him to ask Marika something. 'Did you . . . you know . . . in the back row at the flicks?'

'It always struck me as a stupid place to do it.'

'Whatever it was you could do.'

'Exactly.'

They followed the curve of the balcony toward the open door. When they had almost reached daylight, they passed close to the faun and the curtain in front of the theatre's screen. Abel smelt an acrid dustiness. The curtain was of a faded luteous drabness, but Abel was surprised by the breadth of its pendulous folds.

Marika led him out into the sunshine. They stood now on a skeletal wooden landing from which descended the rungs of a metal stair. Tubular iron rails enclosed the little platform. Through the gaps in the slats at his feet, Abel could see fruit boxes and onion flowers, the land at the back of the building. The paddocks of the countryside began at the back door of the Strand. A little beyond the theatre's hollow plaster, behind the fading gilt and dusty velvet, there had coexisted this second, heavier world, this obdurate and grass-perfumed summer, in which Abel was not altogether disappointed.

'We could do it here,' said Marika. 'There's only those cows could see.' She released Abel's hand and kissed him lightly on the lips. Behind the purplish blueness of her eyes, the narrowing and self-consciousness, he saw opacity and resolution. And when she kissed him lightly, with no apparent passion, he knew her appetite to be at its very keenest.

'Not here,' he said. 'Not now. I'm all played out, I'm sorry. Tell me what you think of Conrad and Electra.'

'The two of them together? They're a bit like us, I suppose. I should really be telling you what I think of us.'

'What *do* you think of us?'

'He doesn't care and she doesn't care. Sheer laziness has brought them together.'

'But us?'

'You're mad about me but you also hate me a bit. You know I'll go away and you know you'll hurt. But you'll harden yourself and become like the rest of the mob. You'll learn what people use sex for.'

'And what's that?'

143

'To remember past lovers. Or forget them.'

'You can't believe that.'

'What are you doing here at Rabbit Bay? When does your life begin? When do you make a start on being an adult?' Her voice lacked stridency; her eyes seemed timid. She stepped away from him and covered her bare navel with her hand. He felt solicitous of the welfare of her skin in the hot light. She turned away and gripped the tubular rail. 'Someone's got to make a living. You think I like working in bloody fucking stack rooms and basements? And Conrad and you. You think it's all beginning but nothing's beginning. I'm very fond of you but I can't *take* you. You just won't do, do you know what I'm saying?'

He felt an inner vertigo, a terror, a fear of homelessness and the unloved condition of the homeless. And he feared losing Marika; he dreaded the stunning boredom of being himself again, of reverting to being alone with himself.

Thirty-seven

We take our punishment and are tough when injury comes. It's only later that we open ourselves to pain; we flower, as it were, belatedly; belatedly the lobes of our dolour open.

Marika came away from the rail. She put her small white fist against my stomach. 'Don't think I don't . . . you know. You really get my attention.' Marika. Marika speaking.

The losing is in the getting. And loss follows loss follows loss. And when we've lost enough, we're ready for death.

'It doesn't matter,' I say. 'I'll have better luck next time.' But I take her fist in my hands and lift it to my lips. What I feel for her one feels only once or twice in a lifetime. How dare we hope to match ourselves to those of whom we have a coded precognition, a genetic expectation? How dare we hope to connect? And those we have the gift of uniquely *seeing* . . . how dare we hope to wed ourselves to them? In a universe of rotating energies, of poised oppositions and elaborate alienations, our chances are nugatory.

I was at my blondest then. I had grown a young man's beard. Marika's hair had a fuzzy, coronal shape. She butted her head gently against my chin.

'I'm peckish,' I said.

'You'll be hungry by the time I get you home.'

'I'll enjoy Electra's roast.'

Re-entering the theatre blinded him for some seconds. The cat was again an obstacle to sure-footed progress, but Abel led Marika back across the dark dress-circle. Before returning to the foyer below, Abel looked once more at the notice on the easel. The film it advertised was personally his: he contained it just as he did the fact of his own birth. He had studied it more exactly than life itself, counting the cuts in certain sequences. If the city was Abel's appropriate habitat, *Il Conformista* belonged to the torrid era he had lived through in Wellington; it belonged to a former, more valid life, to a time of authenticity and courage.

While Abel waited on the pavement outside the milk bar, Marika finished her business inside. When she had emerged from the shop and shut the door, Marika handed Abel a bag of marshmallows.

They had left the township and walked some distance along Pa Road when Abel heard a motorcycle behind them. 'Sounds like an English bike,' he said.

A group of big and ancient macrocarpa shaded this part of the road. The bike passed slowly, idly. Its chromed components reflected the greens and browns through which they moved. This was not a bike to make much noise. His hands resting on high handlebars, the rider wore a helmet of matt black. Bike and rider shared a handsome, erect momentum. The machine was built for the sedate consumption of distance. It seemed to roll forward in dire intimation of its own value. It was a black and polished projectile of many thousands of parts, and its fuel was got in secret from the stars.

On a country road on a Sunday afternoon, it amused Abel to think in these terms. When the bike was a long way off, it turned through a hundred and eighty degrees and began to travel back along the road. As it approached Marika and Abel, it crossed the middle of the road and entered the dusk beneath the trees again. Before the bike was brought to a halt, Abel got an impression of thrust being curbed, of spokes ceasing to tumble. The odours the bike brought into the coolness, of heated oil and metal and sun-warmed chrome, seemed as sweet as the smells from a kitchen.

'You're a show-off,' Abel said.

'That's why I own a bike,' said the rider. Beneath his dull

helmet, Guy Ace wore sunglasses of black opacity. His brown leather jacket was scarred and cracked.

'Let me introduce Marika.'

'Hello,' said Guy in a shy, respectful way. He extended his bare hand and Marika took it.

'Guy's really an old reprobate,' said Abel.

'But a friend, too, I take it,' said Marika.

'I don't get up this way as often as I'd like. It helps to have some sort of destination.'

'Why don't you let Marika show you where the house is?'

It was agreed that Guy would return for Abel. When Marika mounted the pillion of the Triumph, she seemed to think it wise to loop her arms round Guy's waist. The bike left behind a thin blue mist of exhaust. Abel continued to walk toward the sea. The sun was still remarkably high. Abel tended to be irked by the length of summer days: long before they ended he had had enough of them. Some archaic vestige in his brain longed for drizzle and mist and early darkness.

Electra's preparations for dinner were well advanced when Abel arrived at the house on the back of Ace's bike. Guy shed his helmet and jacket and asked where the bathroom was. As Abel was beginning to pour some drinks – to establish a corner of the kitchen bench as a place where drinks could be got – Ace settled himself in Abel's favourite chair. The doors to the patio were open.

'I know your face, of course,' called Electra. 'Abel was talking to you the morning I first met him.'

Guy realised that he was being addressed. 'I've got you now. That's right. I told Abel you looked intelligent.'

'I ended up with his brother. You'll meet Conrad when he comes out of his room.'

'You have family in Wellington?'

'Daddy writes with news of mother's health. It's some very depressing sort of mental trouble. He takes her out but she doesn't respond to that.'

147

Abel handed Guy a glass of watered whisky. 'I had two demons visit me,' said Abel. 'They said they'd raided your garage.'

'And my house.' Guy took a sip of whisky. 'We use the word raid. I seemed to lie in bed and order them about.'

'Bluntcuff and Keys?'

'And others. Bluntcuff took an interest in my shelf of legal texts. One of their Labradors fancied my wife. If they found anything, they didn't tell me.'

'All over the house like that,' said Electra. 'Do we want peas?'

From the pocket of his khaki shirt, Ace pulled a plastic envelope and a book of Rizla cigarette papers. Standing to Guy's left, Abel drank deeply of a mixture of vodka and water. He could see Marika outside. In that part of the garden in which she stood, above the smiling face of the concrete Buddha, the small, carmine heads of some roses showed themselves. Their fragrance carried weakly into the living room. The northern side of the house was now in shadow. Marika's face and clothing registered a diminishment in the ambient light. Yet her blouse seemed to glow, to recommend hers as being a unique spirit.

Using very green material, Guy rolled a joint. Abel poured a second strong vodka. In the coming tussle with dope, Abel would need all he could find in himself of the dour and inflexible; he wanted not to be surprised by sticky, emergent insights. Marika came inside and took the roasting dish from Electra. 'Will you do the gravy? There's a love,' said Electra.

Abel held a gulp of vodka in his mouth. He let it burn his tongue. He felt that he was rehearsing new emotions, feelings strong and negative and painful. It came to him that he was appalled by Marika. *You will rob me of a future* he thought, to see if he really meant it.

He swallowed the vodka. And still he was standing a little

to the left of Guy's elbow. Abel hoped that the look on his face was one of indulgent contentment.

Lincoln strayed into the room. 'That your bike outside?' he asked, at once at home in Guy's company. Because of his friendship with Abel, Guy was known slightly to Lincoln and Conrad. Now Abel was invited to carve the lamb; Electra handed him the carving knife and steel and he crossed into the kitchen to clear a space on the bench in which to work. Before beginning to carve, he drank all the vodka in his glass and poured himself more. The smell of burning New Zealand Green reminded him of the dope's imminence. He decided on two things: he'd be eating little and he wouldn't be smoking.

'Thank God you remembered vinegar, Link,' said Electra. 'You won't mind eating off your knees, Guy? We're all going to have to fend like mad. Conrad can bring another chair from our room.'

Abel made sure that Guy's plate was attractive. He gave his friend, in addition to the boiled peas and roast potatoes and pumpkin, plenty of gravy and sauce. Conrad appeared. When everyone had been served a meal and found a position in which to eat it (the women on the floor and Lincoln at the table on the patio), Guy lit a second joint and handed it to Conrad. As the joint did its rounds, Abel watched settle on the company a somewhat precious silence.

He was the first to finish his meal. In the kitchen, he rinsed his plate under the cold-water tap. Then he retrieved his glass from under the chair he'd vacated, took it to the bench and added more vodka to it.

An orange light clouded the bedroom. The wind-chimes pealed softly as Abel closed the door behind him. Perhaps the sun was setting at last; its rays shone through the transfers Marika had stuck to the window. Chips and smears of colour lay on the bedding, a disassembled spectrum. Abel had almost stopped reading *The French Lieutenant's Woman*. Still, he must think more and feel less. He set his glass on the floor, picked up the book from his pillow and settled back on the bed.

Marika came into the room. 'I'll do the dishes when everyone's finished,' said Abel.

'There's no headlong rush.'

'I just thought I'd do them.'

Marika removed her blouse. Her naked breasts always seemed new to Abel. 'What's the matter?' she asked.

'You. You're the matter.' He put his book aside. 'I thought I'd figured you out. I thought I knew you.'

'You'd feel less grumpy if you smoked some dope.'

'I could do with a new angle on things. What you said this afternoon is beginning to sink in.'

'Not the first time I've said it. Or tried to.'

Apparently looking for some fresh item of clothing, she stooped to her suitcase. Her breasts swayed forward from her ribcage, their whiteness and slight asymmetry striking. Abel saw again what memory could never make complete, those things which seemed to refresh their loveliness while withdrawn from his sight. They tapered; they were full of themselves; their brown nipples were coarse and vigilant. Abel felt his lips pressing against the smoothness of his incisors. Oh, he was, yes, jealous where she was concerned. Her breasts represented the sisterhood of women, and to this sisterhood he was responsible for what became of Marika's happiness. But more than that, even: the thought of her body passing into another man's hands was intolerable to him. He must somehow retain Marika; he must somehow defend and conserve this woman and her breasts.

'Marika, who do you want? What do you want in a man?'

'For the time being, you. You've got what I want in a man.'

'That's really not a very good answer.'

She shrugged and tugged her way into a woollen pullover; when her face appeared through the hole in the top of the garment, it succeeded in looking both blank and silly. 'I'm busy right now,' she said. 'I'm trying to entertain the guest you're neglecting.'

She was stoned and a wee bit drunk: Abel could see that much.

Thirty-eight

Now it was dark outside. Someone had done the dishes. Guy still sat in Abel's armchair. The lamp with the hemispherical white shade had been switched on; as the doors to the patio had not been closed, Abel anticipated an influx of moths. He lit a cigarette at a ring on the gas stove (pink-tipped blue flames: the colours of sunset) and replaced the kettle that had been heating there.

'Have you been asleep?' asked Guy.

'No. No. Just sitting in my room and thinking,' said Abel.

Marika had told him that she was going swimming. Electra was sitting on the floor at Guy's feet; Conrad occupied a straight-backed chair opposite them; the bottle of whisky stood at a point equidistant from each of the men. Abel's wristwatch, at which he had just glanced, gave the time as 9:06.

With more than half the contents of a bottle of vodka inside him, a familiar and pleasant strength was Abel's once more. No. Yes. He had more than subdued his earlier feelings of anxiety and grief. If it had seemed to him that he had lost his emotional capital to mischief and cynicism, he was a man again, for the time being. His mood proceeded from a bodily contentment and was overlaid by a loquacious bravado – not that he was saying anything; not that he had much intention of speaking. Of those present, only Guy could match him: for sheer durability and aplomb, for immunity to the crassness of the world and the corrosive glimmer of chemicals and flesh, only Ace was in *his* league. And beneath it all he was – Abel knew himself to be – one who had mourned already, one who was deeply convinced he was alone.

He was being unfair to Lincoln, of course. It went without saying that Lincoln had qualities. He seemed to understand bodies, did Link. Perhaps because bodies were like machines.

'How's your whisky, Guy?'

'It's good. I'm good, Abel.'

'I don't see Link about.'

'He's gone for a blat on the Triumph,' said Electra.

'Probably half-way to Auckland by now,' said Abel.

'He'd better fucking not be,' said Guy.

'Would you like coffee, Conrad?' Electra asked.

'Not while there's whisky left.' Conrad looked dishevelled and thwarted. 'Plus there's a flagon of sherry in where the pots are kept.'

'Lincoln might be saving that,' said Electra. 'Anyway, you're always as sick as a dog in the morning.'

'And take it out on you, I suppose you'd claim.'

'I'm not saying that, Connie.'

'I can't drink like a man is what you mean. It goes straight to my head is what you think.'

'And so it does. We both know that. And you only drink it when other people provide it.'

'That's charming talk, that is, in front of Guy.'

'He didn't bring anything.'

'He brought the dope.'

'Anyway,' said Electra, contrite and confused, 'I think we're all much happier when there's *no* alcohol and horrible dope in use.'

Abel was touched by Electra's distress but said, 'We don't all carry on like Conrad.'

'So you've got your knife out too,' said Conrad. 'And what do you mean, "carry on"?'

'You become a little vivid and gauche, that's all. You're my brother and I like you so please pipe down.'

The kettle had begun to boil. Abel was standing at the end of the bench. When Electra rose and went into the kitchen, she passed Abel; he scowled and pursed his lips to indicate his sympathy for her, an agreement capable of inflaming the situation. She turned off the gas under the kettle and began to spoon sugar into a large blue mug.

'Have you ever considered the psyche of the surgeon, his psychological profile, Guy?' asked Conrad. 'Electra's dad's a surgeon. Those gloves are like condoms. I bet you can feel the warmth and blood through them. What sort of man wants to spend his mornings up to his elbows in gore? And you'd think he'd have a colleague or two capable of improving his wife's mental health.'

Electra let the spoon fall into the mug. 'Why he does it I just don't know. I try to be good to him.'

'Apologise to the lady, Con,' said Ace, though he had his back to Electra and could not see the tears in her eyes.

'Go fuck yourself.'

'You're looking for a clip.'

'There's nothing I like better than fighting when I'm stoned.'

'The last skinny painter that said that to me . . .'

'Behave yourselves you two,' said Marika. She had come in from the patio and was carrying a towel: this she offered to Electra. To Abel she said, 'Trust you to let things get out of hand.'

'No trouble.' Abel balanced his cigarette on the edge of the bench. Picking up the vodka bottle, he further fortified the mixture of vodka and water in his glass. Marika escorted Electra to her bedroom.

'I fail to see . . .' said Conrad.

'You feed on talking irresponsibly. All right in a pub or something. But a woman is not just one of your mates,' said Guy. 'And to go on about her parents as if they're not always in her thoughts and a source of sadness and worry to her . . . Sadistic ignorance.'

'You think so?'

'Fucking right I think so.'

It was time Abel acted or spoke – on balance he thought it better to act, to move. He extinguished his cigarette in an ashtray and took his glass over to the stereo. Turntable and amplifier stood to the right of the fireplace on a vaguely Mayan platform of bricks and wood – Lincoln's construction. Abel stood his glass on the floor and lifted the transparent lid of the turntable. He set the turntable in motion and moved the head to the fourth track on the first side of the record. *Neil Young* by Neil Young was still the only record in the house.

The air fizzed with that positive lack of sound which precedes the beginning of recorded music. The empty fireplace where the dead bird had lain: when would it next be in use? Abel might be alone in the house when winter came again. And when he turned to face the room once more, he saw that Conrad had left it. Let them all depart, decamp, desert, defect. He had gone to the heart of the material world; he had split the layered world and seen its heart; Marika constituted the core of things but her place was not with him nor his with her. Let them all fuck off and leave him alone, alone to erase his memory of Marika, expunge her articulate image from his mind. But how to deconstruct his idolatry of her when the thought of her crossed legs or the hollows beneath her cheekbones were colourful shadows that glowed behind his forehead, as accessible as stereoscopic slides?

I've been waiting for you
And you've been coming to me
For such a long time now
Such a long time now
  sang Young.

The light from the lamp beside Guy's chair did not much illuminate his face. 'I was looking for a scrap of paper,' he said. The pad Abel kept under the chair rested on his lap. 'What I've got here, this paragraph or stanza – did you write this?'

'There's plenty of blank sheets.'

'If I could write this sort of thing, I'd think I had a talent.'

'Listen to the lyrics of this song. They sound as if they were scrawled on a piece of cardboard. They're crude but they're terrific. They inform.'

Young's words. Marika's words. Marika's particularly were Abel's for keeps: he had a fair collection of them now and they could not be returned to where they had come from. No power or strategy could restore them to the condition of being unsaid.

'There's something going on here, right?'

'You've seen her,' said Abel. 'She makes me feel like a potential strangler.'

'Sunday in the country.'

'I'd forgotten how sordid infatuation was.'

They heard the Triumph being ridden along the track to the back of the house. 'Man,' said Lincoln when he entered the living room, 'that machine is really something.'

'You get your ton?' asked Guy.

'A couple of times. Melston and back in under fifteen minutes.' Lincoln ran a hand through has hair: he'd been riding without a helmet. Guy tore a leaf of paper from the pad on his lap and handed it to Lincoln.

'My number. And address. I'm buying a Norton. You might like to help me work on it.'

Abel was at ease among men. The cogs of masculine intercourse were visible. One acknowledged what one saw and measured oneself against it. Lincoln's sexual enjoyment of Abel – and his of Lincoln – had made not the slightest difference to their relationship; how could that be explained, unless in terms of the deepest mutual respect, of the most settled trust?

'There's plenty of moonlight,' said Lincoln. 'I think I'll take a dip.'

When he went to ask who wanted to go swimming, only Electra returned to the room with him. Though holding her Tyrolean doll, she was dressed in a white bikini. Her limbs looked very brown in the lamplight; Abel was struck by how much of her was leg. She placed Sigmund on the bench and drew a towel around her shoulders.

'I must remember to sew him,' she said. 'His eye's coming loose.'

9:37.

Thirty-nine

A moth circled the lamp. It cast a theatrical shadow. Lincoln and Electra left the house and Abel closed the doors to the patio.

Fifteen minutes elapsed. When Lincoln returned he was running. He had to bang on the glass to be let in. 'She's vanished,' he gasped when Abel had opened the door. 'I think Electra's sunk.'

The three men ran to the beach. Abel led in the sprint through the dunes and was the first to reach the water's edge. 'Electra?' he called. 'Electra!'

He located her towel and stood near that. An aqueous light of yellow and rose tinted the southern part of the sky. It was as if the sun had retreated to the very back of a cavern in which day was eternal. The moon's snowy globe made the sea shine like a dye of the most radiant blue, the blue of china or fire or of a butterfly's wing. The tide appeared to be turning; the sea was almost at rest. Wavelets broke timidly on the sand, creating an appearance of shallowness, a belief that the sea as a whole lacked any depth. To drown in all that calm would surely be a feat, Abel thought. These were the waters of dream or imagination. Serenity and silence had swallowed Electra. What one had here was the theft of something living. What one had here was magic of a kind.

'I've called and called,' said Lincoln. 'I've swum and fucking swum and she's not there.' He was panting and moving his jaw from side to side, his hands on his knees. The moonlight made his body look pale and cold. Abel touched him on the shoulder and felt roundness, the thickness of a muscle sheathing bone. Lincoln's flesh was as warm as the air.

'That's good,' said Abel, 'you've done very well.'

'She could have climbed out and gone home,' said Guy – with no apparent conviction.

'Any rip or undertow?' Abel asked.

'No rip. No undertow,' Lincoln said. 'A slight current that might have carried her south.'

Had the partnership of fatigue and intoxication put her to sleep in the water? Her insensible head could be seen in a dozen places. Abel glimpsed Electra's water-blackened hair amid the lift and tilt of the sea's facets, between the spangles riding the ripples; he saw it where there was darkness, a robust illusion lasting only an instant.

'There's a local cop,' said Abel.

'You think he'll have a boat?' Lincoln asked.

'The cop should be told,' said Guy. 'The cop should be brought here.'

'You'd better go and get him,' Abel said.

Guy jogged off toward the silver dunes. Nothing in nature flinched. Moon and sand and sea were undiminished; they waited for an event to complete itself. The sound of the tide turning, of wavelets collapsing feebly, was all that could be heard.

'I'd better front Conrad.'

'I'll keep an eye out here,' Lincoln said.

I felt no need to rush back to the house. The noise of the Triumph's motor being started reached me as I crossed the beach. I knew that I was afraid of confronting Conrad. Entering the house from the patio, I went to the glass I had left on the kitchen bench. Even as I downed the sour vodka, the strange simplicity of what was taking place began to sober me.

I heard the toilet flush. Marika came into the kitchen. She put a hand behind her head and stretched. 'It's been a long hot day.'

'Yes, I said, 'it has.'

'You're not *still* drinking?'
'We think Electra's drowned.'
'My God, Abel.'
'We can't be sure yet.'
'Isn't there . . . Shouldn't there . . .'
'Guy's gone for the local policeman. I'll speak to Conrad.'

This was a moment from which there was no exit except in going forward. I didn't want to stand before my brother and move my lips in speech. It was as if I had something to be ashamed of. My mouth had become a proboscis, an instrument of invasive penetration; my mouth could only despoil and impoverish.

Conrad had made an attempt to get into bed. He hadn't undressed and the sheets covered only his middle. The room was uncommonly untidy. With Lincoln's help, Conrad had equipped himself with a defeated old table on the top surface of which he mixed his pigments. The empty whisky bottle stood on this. I smelled whisky and socks, turpentine and linseed oil.

'Why have you turned on the light?' Conrad asked.
'To wake you up. Electra's missing, Con.'

He didn't open his eyes. 'Can't have got far. We'll get in the van and look. I'll fetch her back. She means more to me than you think. I'll bring her home.'

'Lincoln thinks she's drowned.'
'On a night like this? Impossible.'
'I think you'd better get up.'

He was going to be slow to do that. Marika said she would take him a cup of coffee. I returned to the beach. A hundred yards from where I had left Lincoln, I caught up with him and fell into step beside him. 'This is a weird fucking number,' he said.

The sea was to our right and we were walking south. A ridge of froth ran along the sand. We had not gone far when we came upon Electra. In the copious light of the moon, her tan looked very dark. She lay face down in an inch or two of water. Her bikini's white thongs seemed to truss and package her body.

Forty

100 yards = 91.4400 metres. I think in terms of yards and feet and inches. At the very least, I think in terms of an obsolete system of measurement.

After as much as forty-five minutes, people dragged from the sea have been resuscitated, brought back to a state of viability and consciousness.

We pulled Electra far enough to remove her from the water. Then Lincoln and I knelt down on the moist sand. Electra lay on her side. Lincoln thrust two fingers into her mouth, moved them about and withdrew them. Satisfied that she was still not breathing, we rolled her onto her back. Lincoln covered her mouth with his and expelled four full breaths of air. I watched his fingers feel for the pulse of her carotid artery.

'No breathing or pulse,' he murmured. 'Can you compress her heart?'

It was a technique I'd seen demonstrated beside the chlorine-reeking pool in which I'd learned to swim. It could be applied to dummies, to flesh-coloured mock-ups of the human thorax. It could be applied with hope of a feigned response to nubile and complaisant human actors.

Lincoln breathed and blew until a film of sweat had formed on his forehead and shoulders. I pushed and pressed until my wrists were sore. We laboured for five or ten or fifteen minutes.

'How long have we been at this?'

'I'm beginning to think it's useless,' Lincoln said. His fingers sought a pulse in Electra's neck.

I had heard the noise of the Triumph a long way off. Now it sounded closer, sharp and steady in its return through stillness, through the peaceful country night. Without getting very much louder, the noise ceased. A diffuse cloud of white illumination appeared above the place where Pa Road ended. Then the lights of a car shot out to sea, not touching the water. Soon they were extinguished. A less robust quiet visited the beach for a moment. I heard the car door slam and Guy's voice raised in direction or enquiry.

Electra didn't seem particularly dead. Lincoln took his hand away from her throat. When he stood up, he did so slowly. He stood above me and brushed the sand from his knees and shins.

Accident is visible, conspicuous: Guy Ace and the policeman jogged toward us as if toward the crimped, hoisted bonnets and cross-eyed ferocity of collision. As I stood up, the masterful strangeness of authority took over; the constable went down on one knee beside the body, obscuring Electra's rinsed and neutral face.

Conrad had not come down to the beach; though I was glad of this, I couldn't imagine what extremity of sloth or callousness was preventing him. Guy was dispatched by the cop to get blankets. Lincoln and I became bystanders; we were excluded from the routine of official discovery and attendance. A doctor arrived whose drowning this became, a tidal phenomenon to be dealt with nimbly, to be sampled, as it were, with trousers rolled. (He was wearing bicycle-clips.) When Guy returned from the policeman's car, the cop shone his torch on the blankets Guy had brought: they were of the blood-red sort carried in ambulances. The constable took a blanket from the stack and he and the doctor covered Electra's corpse.

It was not yet midnight. The cop was a tall young man in summer uniform. The doctor wore Benjamin Franklin specs and his jacket had leather patches on the elbows. We were all standing now.

I put a blanket round Lincoln's shoulders. 'There's a husband of sorts,' I said. 'My brother will have to be told.'

'I'll do that,' said Guy. He winked at me grimly.

163

'And parents?' the doctor suggested.

'We're not on the phone out here.'

'I'll be taking you into town,' the cop told me. 'You can ring her people from my office.'

'An autopsy is usual in these cases,' said the doctor. 'The body will have to go through to Melston. There's an ambulance on its way.' He was in his early sixties. 'They say that drowning's not an altogether unpleasant experience. They say . . . but never mind.'

They say our cells remember their primordial conception, the brine in which they formed when life began on this planet. A puddle of tepid water, a wriggling sliver of life: our spines have memories. But I had seen Electra's face for the last time – sealed, closed off, gently impervious to the moving shadows of further experience. Drenched but drying. Finished.

The doctor would stay with the deceased. Attaching myself to the cop submissively, I followed him across the beach and climbed to the police car. A connoisseur of slowness, the constable drove with idle watchfulness. His short-sleeved shirt gave off the freshness of the hearty family wash. A marred, unhappy holiday was over. The nervousness I'd brought to Rabbit Bay had proved to be abiding: the licence and voyeurism of vacation – nakedness at breakfast; the aphrodisiac of sand between the toes – had not been enough to block reality, to stifle my preoccupation with all that was exterior and gloomy. Nor, for the present, was I thinking about Marika, including her in my evaluation of this rained-off match, this suspended competition. There was pain and further hurt (stacked darkness and piled worry) in that direction too.

I sat beside a desk. The office had an empty fireplace. When I had made my statement, I swore to its veracity on a Bible. The constable told me that talking to Lincoln would complete his enquiries. It's worse when it's a little kid, he said. His forearms bore many fine blond hairs. I missed my vocation, I thought: touching distress with order is a man's proper function. In another room the policeman's children slept, buoyant and undrowned, their soft hair dry.

The clock on the wall advanced its second-hand. Was it too late to ring a noted surgeon? On the contrary: there was too much earliness in everything; earliness evinced itself in the glare of fluorescent tubes, in the absence of stubble from the policeman's jaw.

I opened the appropriate telephone book. The father's number stuck out like a forced card. With the cop's shrugged permission, I rang Tolls and heard the call being placed. In a bedroom or a kitchen in Karori . . .

Electra's mother answered.

'Is Mister Begg available?' I asked.

'Shall I say who's calling?' Her voice was colourful, a fattened version of Electra's.

'My name's Abel Blood. It might mean something to him.'

His was a cordial baritone. 'You've been mentioned in dispatches,' he said.

'There's a cop here with me. I've got unpleasant news.'

'Something's happened on the road?'

'Electra's been drowned, Mister Begg.'

'I'm very sorry to hear it,' said Stephen Begg.

'She went to the beach late this evening. There was someone swimming with her. He didn't see or hear anything.'

'Has her body been recovered?'

'Her body's been recovered.'

'I'm glad of that. I thank God for that.' There carried up the line the friction of flesh against plastic. 'My daughter was an epileptic. Few people knew. She was also deeply ashamed of her condition.'

'I'll tell the constable.'

'She didn't like to take her medication. Epileptics, schizophrenics . . . They have that in common, it seems.'

Forty-one

When the body had been removed from the beach, Guy and Lincoln retired to the house. Lincoln went to his caravan. Guy found Marika and Conrad in the living room and made a pot of tea. Little was said until Abel returned from the police station.

Guy reported the few events that had taken place. 'The ambulance bloke was a woman,' he offered.

'I feel for Lincoln,' said Abel. 'He worked very hard to bring Electra back.' His eyes were on Conrad. 'Her father's coming tomorrow. I don't know why. He's driving up to Melston and stopping here.'

'It's tomorrow already,' said Conrad. He had been weeping.

'Did you know that she had fits?' Abel asked him.

'Moments of agitation or absence. They didn't seem to qualify as fits.'

'But you thought her swimming was a good idea?'

'What did I have to do with it? She knew herself. She knew her own condition.'

'Her father said she was ashamed of it.'

'She was ashamed, all right. Ashamed and afraid. Now all she is is some flesh and blood and bones. And a ghost, of course, a little bit of a ghost. She's joined all the others. I can't get over it. How long will it take? How long will it take me to get over it?'

Marika was standing near Conrad; she bent to the chair in which he was sitting and took his head in her arms and kissed his brow. Abel was moved by her concern for his brother, glad he was there to see it; Marika seemed to extend herself, to reveal a new function, to double her identity.

The flagon of sherry remained in the pot cupboard. It was 2:00 am before Conrad was ready to face the emptiness of his room and his bed. The unshaven man with grubby cheeks had been given a new life. Void and resonant, valueless and tinny, it was impossible to decline. In tears again, Conrad asked Guy Ace to join him, to sleep on the floor in the room where madness waited.

In bed beside Marika, Abel wondered: wonder pulsed before his open eyes; black wonder almost audible beset him. 'He's an orphan again,' he told her.

Her fingers gently hefted his balls. Now that Conrad and he were men (if that was what they were), his brother's anguish had moved to the other end of the house. Aunt Ellen's tread could not be heard in the hall. Conrad's fidelity to those who had died exhausted and levelled him. His beautiful mothers were never coming home.

The shut-eyed blank of it. The comfortless black fact of death's big negative. Death was there with Abel in the dark. Why was one brought to life and given a body if only in order to be returned to deadness? Electra had been retracted, whisked backward like a mistake into non-being.

Blood-warm air was trapped beneath the sheets; Abel rolled toward Marika through the odour of their flesh. He felt his penis leaning out of himself, tugging at its restraints like a weight about to fall. And he teetered with it. *Use it do it use it* Marika seemed to whisper. Her vagina was wet; he entered her easily. As often as he fucked her, the proportions of her body seemed to vary. Now, almost all the depth of her pelvis was filled by his cock. Did Marika enjoy him as much as he did her? So strong was his need for intimacy, he wanted to eat her teeth.

Abel slept badly. At length he became aware of a fungal whiteness, the first dim light of day. He got out of bed and pulled on his jeans. Marika continued to sleep. Her shoulder was bare; the pale tints from the transfers on the window lay on her arm like mood or thought – abstractions. She was immortal, of course: *she* could not be taken, unless by means of great brutality, inhuman depredation. He felt his fondness for her in his nostrils, in a yawning of the membranes.

Guy was in the kitchen. The kettle was on the boil.

'I need some speed,' said Abel.

'I can offer you a smoke.'

'If Electra's father's coming I need to be awake. I want to be able to mutter my sympathy.'

'You don't feel any?'

'Of course I do, believe me, but it's not just charity that begins at home.'

Guy took a cup of tea along the hall to Conrad. Abel looked at his watch. Away from Wellington and the markets, he was seldom awake at six. He was overhung and ahead of himself; there was something of Christmas morning in the hour, the air.

Guy sat in a chair near the foot of Conrad's bed. Conrad was sitting up, his cup on the paint-smeared table nearby.

'How are you feeling?' asked Abel.

'I shouldn't drink whisky. Anything but whisky.'

'I won't argue with that.'

'She asked me to go to the beach with her. What am I *like* when I'm pissed? I want to go and find her and look at her.' He hung his head and shook. When he could speak again, he said, 'She's just had a whole night of being dead. It can't really be grasped. She's lying in a morgue with her face all blank. I want to say goodbye. I want to know she's gone.'

'Drink your tea,' said Guy.

'I'd like a cigarette.'

Abel left the house. A mass of grubby cloud tented the land. There were warmth, windlessness. Over the sea to the west, the sky was visible in greenish streaks. A familiar haze was in place, the russet dust from a distant conflagration. Australia was on fire.

Gaining Pa Road, Abel turned toward the beach. He halted when he was abreast of the copse of pines. The trees knew nothing of mishap, of upset and confusion. And Abel could see a bird. With swollen throat and pebble-coloured breast, the thrush delivered a penetrating song, attentive to the theme it was disclosing. Abel didn't doubt that there was beauty in the world; the trick was in being untroubled enough to enjoy it.

Stephen Begg arrived at ten o'clock that morning. Abel had been talking to Lincoln; emerging from the caravan he saw a car pass down Pa Road. A minute later a man appeared on the track. He was youthful, tall and dressed in a three-piece suit; his shirt was blue and he wore a scarlet tie. The eyes and mouth, advancing, seemed to trespass, to stray familiarly from a state of quarantine: Electra had taken after her father.

As Abel shook hands with the surgeon, Lincoln came to the door of the caravan. Begg looked up at him. 'I don't want you chaps feeling bad about things,' said Begg.

'This is Lincoln Dorne. Lincoln really did do all he could.'

'I'm sure you're all very bitterly distressed.'

They went into the house and were met by Marika. She told Begg her name.

'And did you and Electra become friends?' he asked.

'I like to think we did.'

'I'm sure of it and very glad you did. Electra hoped you would. She hadn't had much happiness. Her mother and I are grateful that she found friends.'

Abel was anxious that Conrad should show himself. As Marika served tea, Begg said, 'I'm sorry that my wife was unable to come.'

'She sounded well on the phone,' Abel said.

'I think she's well, myself. And then I see that she's not.'

Conrad came into the living room. Sandwiched between

his hands was a shallow pile of folded paper sheets. He was wearing the paint-soiled trousers he worked in, but his hair was wet and shaped and marked by the comb.

'I've had to put some of her things in a box. You always seem to leave with more than you brought. This is her sheet music. I never really heard her play. I suppose I've been a bit negligent.'

Begg extended his ringless technician's hand. 'Conrad? Are you Conrad?'

'I wish I could give you her. I wish I could return her.'

Forty-two

As if in a spirit of experiment, rain had begun to fall. Drops of rain were marking the patio. Fat drops of rain were turning themselves into dark gashes on the bricks. I thought of eggs breaking; I thought of eggs and wounds shaped like daggers.

And in the garden a rustling, a slow patter. Already rain was beading the sheen on Begg's Mercedes. I had liked and pitied him. The pores of his face knew the astringency of Old Spice. He departed like a bachelor diplomat, poised and stoical. But I had thought him human, consummately so. Electra's funeral (a cremation, he guessed) could only follow the coroner's release of her body. He would be in touch.

I'd decided not to go to work. While Marika was in another room, I lay on the bed and attempted to read. Rain was falling steadily now on garden and house. The gutters above the eaves were brimming and burdened. Over road and beach and sea rolled a silver translucency. The local lemons would be glinting like things dunked.

My narrative collapses in post-coital fashion. In order to make a single point cogent, I forego the expression of others.

When Evan arrived I saw

When Evan came his hands

The wetness we made together was pooled beneath her buttocks. I knew it was past midnight. Someone knocked on our bedroom door.

'There's a bloke here to see you,' Lincoln hissed through the wood.

I wiped myself on the sheet and put on underpants. Monday's rain had done nothing to lessen the heat. The day had passed in idleness and tension, Guy dispensing ganja like medicine to a band of despondent lepers. One had felt the botanical realm swelling, plants growing so gigantic and fleshy as to resemble those in a painting by Rousseau.

'What do you want?' I asked the figure in the hall.

'Come out to the truck,' said Evan. The reek of his drinking filled the darkness.

'Come out to the truck? Why the fuck would I want to come out to the truck?'

'There's stuff I want you to see.'

'Oh, Evan, no, don't *tell* me. For fuck's sake, Evan, *no*.'

'I got the lot. It was easy.'

I drew him into the bedroom and switched on the light. Marika yelped and covered her head with a blanket. Evan looked almost sober. The blood had withdrawn from the flesh at the sides of his nostrils; his face had been built around a blurred fusion of sedation and arousal.

'There's no one with you?' I asked.

'I did it on my own. It was only a box on the wall like an ordinary cupboard.'

'A cupboard like a box. You're excited.'

'It busted open easy enough.'

I had to see what he had. And what he had he'd brought straight to my door. I was already implicated, endangered. His spoils could not be simply wished away. Their very propinquity was energising.

I sent Evan out to his truck. He returned to the bedroom with a large paper bag of the sort you got from a bottlestore.

'Shift your legs,' I said to Marika.

Evan emptied his cornucopia. Of flowers, fruit and corn. For from his bag slithered a litter of valuables, the glassy products of remote laboratories. Each white container and polished bottle represented a process of ingenious synthesis or careful reduction to essence. The labels of these things made an alphabet on the bed, an abstruse new script which eyes like mine could read. Let me see. Here were tincture of opium and crystals of cocaine. There were ampoules of adrenaline and bottles of Benzedrine and Dexedrine tablets. Here were discs of Omnopon in flat-bottomed tubes. Mention must also be made of the boxed cards of my old stand-by, Palfium. I'm talking here about a collection of *items*; I'm noting their see-through gleam and icy shine. But they seemed to me to be possessed of the trick potency of toys, of gadgets. Their labels bore the stamp of the printer's craft (expiry date and maker's logotype), the bottles the pimply ridges of industry's numerology. Morphine sulphate and morphine hydrochloride shaped themselves to the walls of their brown jars; I knew that theirs was really a bounteous Persil whiteness.

Evan looked pleased with himself.

'You want to know what to do?' I asked him. 'You want to know what to do with morphine in this quantity?'

'I knew you'd know. Tell me.'

'Throw it off a cliff is what. Are you half-pissed or something? Are you half-mad or something?'

'You've got to take risks in life.'

'Criminals and fools,' moaned Marika, turning onto her stomach.

The morphine alone stood for money. While money stood for trouble. All the drugs in the world, from alcohol on down, were stockpiled by canny barons, appropriated and priced, kept from the people who couldn't stump up with the cash. In short, made fortunes from. A bottle of gin was a symbol, or a packet of cigarettes – that which addicted was already spoken for. And this broad web of ownership was policed, kept tight and legitimate by men in suits from carpeted homes, athletic strangers to pain, their encephalins and endorphins flowing, axons and dendrites sparking. They had access to boats and spry helicopters. I tried to picture the hospital Evan had visited with his misdirected energy, his wrenching. I saw roses and tiled roofs, white globes like moons. Even now a mufti car

173

would be parked on hospital gravel, its radio leaking that underwater talk, that helium-squeezed quacking.

There was time: it was night. For those who stay awake, the night is full of time, of hours in which to *do*.

'I want you to leave here now,' I told Evan. 'I want you to go home and go to bed. When you surface at ten or eleven, you'll remember what you've done and begin to feel dread and nausea. That's when some of these pharmaceuticals might come in handy, but you won't have them any more.'

'I didn't use my key. I made it look like a normal burglary.'

'Good for you. Go home.'

'But you'll owe me a favour.'

'I'll owe you a what?'

'You'll owe me a favour. *You* know.'

'Look. Evan. My friend. I'll owe you a smack in the head is what I'll owe you.'

Conrad was sleeping the sleep of the spent, the hopelessly bereaved. In sleep we are immortal; we stalk a landscape in which appearances mutate, but the subconscious mind never dreams its own death.

I was able to wake Guy without disturbing my brother. 'You'd better come with me,' I whispered.

I put the bottles, packets and plastic containers back in the bag they had come in and took them to the living room. Then I dressed and turned out the light in the bedroom.

Forty-three

'The tincture of o is difficult to use. You have to somehow burn off the alcohol.'

'And?'

'And the coke isn't suitable for snorting. You might be able to crush it but you'd still have your basic ground glass,' said Guy. He was sitting in Abel's chair and had switched on the lamp. The drugs were arrayed on the floor in front of him.

There wouldn't be time to enjoy them. In the presence of this smooth contraband, Abel knew himself to have the potential for ineptitude, for grave solecism. He felt a strong disinclination to handle any of the objects again. Indeed, to touch them at all without gloves was probably unsafe, the equivalent of logging on to any investigation of their theft. And of Evan's deed there was something amounting to the tasteless infringement of universal taboo, the desecration of consecrated vessels, of inviolable space.

He took the flagon of sherry from under the sink, opened it and poured himself a drink. 'That stuff has to be moved. It has to be got rid of.'

'I agree,' said Guy.

'Will you have a glass of plonk?'

'I think I will.'

'What about the morphine?'

'It's just what the doctor ordered. In fact, if I had a syringe . . .'

'But you're uneasy about it?'

'Bluntcuff and Keys have been busy. There's holes in the network.'

'I know a man called Omar Kidd,' said Abel.

'Do you know where to find him?'

In a mushroom-coloured cell. At the top of a flight of steps. 'He gave me a number once. I might just have kept it.'

Abel returned to the bedroom and woke Marika. 'I'm sick of this. I want to sleep,' she said.

'Look after Conrad. Please. Guy's going to Wellington and I'm going with him.'

'But there's all this muddle and everything.'

'I'll try to get back smartly.' He kissed her on the lips. A warmth came off her breasts – a warm, mammary odour – and he felt her fingers on the nape of his neck.

'What if the police come here?'

'Say I'm on a bender,' he said. 'Say I have a bent for disappearing.'

Against the skirting-board near his side of the bed lay the little satchel in which he kept odds and ends. Among the envelopes and paper-clips, he found the telephone number. He was reminded of the continental sevens Kidd made, had pressed with a pencil into the gloss of the card.

Guy Ace had dressed. He'd returned the bottles, packets and plastic containers to their paper bag. All but one. 'Ritalin,' said Guy. 'For personal use.' He slipped the bottle into his jacket and zipped up the pocket. Then he swallowed the tablet lying on his tongue and drank a mouthful of sherry.

'I think I'll stick to the plonk,' Abel said. 'I'm in a plonk sort of mood.' He felt, moreover, a readiness to sweat, to suffer misgivings.

'We'll have to take the bike. I suggest we wait until there's traffic on the roads.'

'I'm sure you'll keep me amused.'

Speed made Abel garrulous, suggestible, defenceless. It made him wickedly, if harmlessly, mendacious; it made him weirdly inventive and accident-prone. He wondered how the Ritalin would affect Guy. His own mood was one of clearheadedness, of purposeful detachment. And he wanted to be responsible, to remain morally wakeful, to feel his scruples touched, even abraded. From any collective opinion or action, he always dissented; with a sad sense of exclusion, he dissented. He was about to do something necessary. He would be almost alone in doing it. For once, he didn't dissent, he was not at odds: he would save a youngster's bacon – heroically.

He waited for dawn. No wind pressed the walls of the house or lifted the leaves in the garden. He wished that rain was falling on the black patio. He wished that there were curtains he could draw to hide the lamp and the light it threw on Guy and himself. *A little while, and you will see me no more.* The words were those of a durable and melancholy song, some lines of tough old poetry not yet complete, not yet fully assembled and identified. Shakespeare? Milton? No. *Again a little while, and you will see me.* A bit of a let-down, really that last bit. John's words were graven, Roman, slots through which there showed like sky the epic. Their meaning was their sound, the music of resignation and retreat, of heart-broken defeat.

He waited for there to be traffic on the highway.

Forty-four

I talked to Lincoln Dorne a week or two ago. He had had all his teeth out and was waiting for dentures. He's married and working in 'the industry', constructing sets and rigging explosions. Our respective memories seemed to me discrete, retroactively selective, privately concerned with different things. He thought he'd heard that Ace was living in Tasmania.

Here in the present are the static and the sure, a cat lapping its bit of curried mince, a ragged stencil of sunlight on warm planks. An eviction notice lies under the silver bar on my typewriter.

Claude Hebron is dead. At sixty-five. They've published that old photograph – the panama and beard. I see that he was born in Illinois. (Why should I have such a clear idea of Illinois, what Illinois is like? It's a rounded black car bonnet, pointy and female; it's a patch of earthen road and a clear sky. Illinois is a dusty warmth in the mouth.) I don't expect you've read him – no one's read him. But I like the way he works on the page, his trial-and-error style of doing things, his admission of the reader to his workshop. He learned that the sphere of male homosexual practice is for those in retreat from the real. That the real, like it or not, is the heterosexual.

The rectum is not a sexual organ. Think how mechanically unsatisfactory is any masculine attempt at coupling. I've always been repelled by the notion of anal intercourse. I have a mental block about bumming. Bumming is my stumbling-block – a bumming-block, perhaps. I won't be bummed. I just can't be bummed. But in sexual matters I'm never confused; where desire is concerned, I'm never in any doubt. I find beauty where

I shouldn't. I'm often ambushed by looks; my eye is surprised. And it's in and with the eye that we sin: the eye is the fly in our ointment.

When Lincoln and I were together that time, that once, in him or in me or between us was Marika: Marika was included and satisfied.

It must be obvious to you by now that this is all a mistake, my writing at such length a gauche and risible error. I can only answer that the celibate have time on their hands, that the abstinent are suckers for things to do. (And whence the implication in the words 'celibate', 'abstinent', of volition, of choice?) I'm disengaged and idle, a greasy shaft. I'm waiting to be tripped into rotation, but I may wait forever. For at the most dry and candid level of myself, in my most sober but unflinching heart, I know I'm in a condition of retraction or withdrawal, a state which confers a bleak social abeyance.

I'm in retreat from Marika. I'm in retreat from Marika and the women who followed her. (I blot and erase to keep the fear from my tone; my Bic sketches blocks of obliteration.) There was even a time when I inflicted pain, the Jew turned crypto-Nazi interrogator, when I made sure I was not the first to grieve. But now I baulk at entering the ring; I'm loath to begin the grappling. I shrink from the cruel mystery of Marika, of womanhood. Is man a simian dimwit or a god that he remembers with tearful gratitude a state of famished dependence?

To want, to moon and yearn . . . There'll be few more provocations.

If Guy is living in the lushness of

Forty-five

Above the dismal clutter of Paekak', its flammable wooden huddle and oily timbers, clouds which seemed to partake of flame, of the hues of smoke and fire, khaki and peach and puce.

They were in Wellington by seven. Here the sky was clear. Guy Ace reduced the speed of the Triumph. Jervois Quay seemed very wide and clean, its surface battleship-grey. The iron uprights of the fences along the wharves made a twinkling disclosure of the harbour. The sun cast chips of brilliance on the sea.

The few drinks he'd had – his sleeplessness and mild intoxication – sat well with Abel. Returning to the city on the back of a bike was his idea of a pleasure, a release. He felt responsible and competent. And all he saw from the pillion was good, touched by significance.

Outside Guy's garage on Mount Victoria, Abel dismounted. He held the stiff and bulky paper bag. A sere strip of flax lay in the gutter. He watched Guy lean the Triumph into a balanced attitude of rest. Guy flourished keys. They entered the garage through the small door in the larger.

The four-paned goblins' window provided a meagre light. Pale nether stalks were pressed to its glass. The men stood beneath the root-threaded mantle of the earth. Abel and Guy were electricians: they worked with cables and colour-coded wires in spooky shafts and tunnels and glowing wells.

Guy found a small backpack, a thing with padded straps and Velcro seals. He tossed it at Abel. 'Put the morphine in that. I'll look after the rest.'

'So be it.' So be it. 'I'll walk to the corner in a minute. I'll try that number I've got.'

Abel put the two fattest jars in the backpack and hefted the bundle for weight. There was none to speak of. And the bag or kiddie's pack or whatever it was continued to look empty. He laid it on the floor and quit the garage in a mood of busy contentment. He walked in sunshine freely, conventionally employed. There was a telephone box outside the dairy. Its gleaming, thick red paint seemed to run.

A brass finger-plate. An off-white telephone. He fed the apparatus a coin. He dialled the number with fancy sevens. Against the sill of the dairy was propped the flat wire cage of a *Dominion* billboard.

'Who's this?' demanded Kidd.

Abel gave his name.

'I'm ill,' said Kidd. 'I'm sick.'

'The police are looking for you.'

'I know that perfectly well. It's not your place to tell me.'

'I think we can transact a little business.'

'I'm finished. I'm sick. I can't operate.'

CANADIAN ADRIFT 17 DAYS said the billboard.

'I helped you out, once.'

'Of course you did,' said Kidd. 'I'm forgetting my manners. I'm forgetting myself. There's no pain, as such. Just this dizzying feeling of being on the brink of extinction.'

When Abel returned to the garage, Guy handed him a coffee. 'He'll meet me,' Abel said. 'He's having peculiar turns but he'll meet me.'

Abel carried the backpack, his finger hooked through a nylon loop. Guy took nothing. He locked the garage and mounted the Triumph. Abel got aboard. The bike coasted and skimmed – along the edge of the queued morning traffic, down toward the lights at Courtenay Place.

Abel waited for Kidd by the iron gates of the wharf. A drinking-fountain was set against the wall of a nearby building.

181

Abel thought it resembled a baptismal font. His Uncle Athol had known a story about it, one Abel couldn't recall. But the foundation commemorated the life of a dog, an habitué of ships and of these wharves. Perhaps that was story enough.

Our pasts are fabrications.

Now Omar Kidd was touching Abel's elbow. Abel looked toward Jervois Quay and saw a taxi departing. As if to protect him from the sun, Kidd was wearing his fawn trench coat. The shirt was lemon with a pattern of tiny cherries.

'You look pale,' said Abel.

'It's a paroxysmal tachycardia. One minute I'm fine, the next . . . There's a pill that puts the ticker on track again.'

'You're all right at the moment?'

'They say it won't kill me. Sometimes I wish it would. Shall we walk?'

'Your coat needs dry-cleaning.'

'And you need a lesson in tact.'

'A detective showed me your photograph. You looked like a film star with cancer.'

They walked on in silence, in full sunlight now, past hawsers and crates and drying nets, through salt air and odours of the sea. 'I'm right under their noses,' said Kidd. 'In defence of a certain paradigm, I've worked myself to a frazzle. But I stay put at the centre of things, still and invisible.'

'What paradigm is that?'

'One according to which the natural man is promoted, not imprisoned. One according to which the rich are eaten.'

'Oh. That one.'

'So what have you got for me?'

'Morphine sulphate and morphine hydrochloride.'

'How much?'

'Don't ask me the weights. But jars of it, big jars.'

'And you want no more to do with these big jars?'

'That's roughly it.'

'There's a rust bucket ahead. You'll come aboard with me.'

Forty-six

Kidd's was a switched and skewed ethic, a whore's mirror-image morality. (She doesn't fuck her friends. She doesn't kiss her tricks.) And taped to the riveted bulkhead, Marc Chagall. His *Artist's Portrait with Seven Fingers*.

I'm in the market for assurance of my value, physical assurance of my physical worth. I like that long-legged blonde of the posters; I want the Bendon model and the gal touting Levis. Let someone approach. Give me that subtle imminence, that lissom arrival, that svelte imposition of gesture and expression. There can be something dire in an eyebrow. I need a woman with what I dare not think about. I lack the ultimately personalised girlfriend, her slight shoulders and ribs and scented cheek. Marika had push and pull: her presence constituted a field, a darting web of forces. And her unthinking fidelity to herself operated on others like a moral authority. Nor was she particularly robust, her lake-blue eyes purblind and straining to see. She saw, nonetheless. But what is belief in her without her?

Forty-seven

Yellowing, cloacal, the ship's name could be read on her bow. Abel followed Kidd up a cleated gangplank. Much of Kidd's tallness was in his legs. He had the high, jutting buttocks of a black man.

The *Sea Snake* was rusty, stained and redolent – as if of flora dredged from the bottom of the sea. It was a tighter, more metallic place than any Abel was used to. He sensed oil and sand beneath his shoes.

There was no one about. Stored and radiated by iron and wood, the heat on deck was already intense. Kidd led Abel aft. They entered a dark mess, airy and cool, through whose open portholes the sky was visible in vivid discs. The central table almost filled the cabin. In the middle of the table, small wooden rails formed a rectangle. Penned by these rails were bottles of sauce and condiment. There were black sauce, tomato, HP and soya.

Abel put the backpack on the table. 'You don't look well, Omar.'

'I took a tablet before I came out. It fixed me almost at once. The heart begins to race, God knows why. Your blood pressure falls. Life seems to fade and begin to slip away. Your heart races like a clock gone berserk and you wait for it to fail.' Kidd indicated the backpack. 'Tell me how you came by this stuff.'

Abel did so.

'And the girl who plays the piano?'

Abel told him.

'She carried a doll about, poor soul.'

'I don't want money,' said Abel. 'I don't know why I didn't just flush this shit.'

'I liked Electra. And I like you. It would seem you've got a lot on your plate.'

He sat down at the end of the table. The glare from a porthole lit one side of his face. He opened the backpack and withdrew the jars of morphine, standing them upright on the table before him. Sellotaped to the bulkhead near his shoulder was a page torn from a cheap magazine. Reproduced on the thin paper was a painting by Chagall.

Kidd looked up at Abel, one half of his face in light. Abel saw a pitted, cellular skin. 'My health has caused me to take an early retirement.'

'From what?' Abel asked.

'It's time for me to cast off a disguise.'

'You're going to burn the coat?'

'I could tell you the outfit I belonged to, the department within the branch, the cell within the department, but you wouldn't relish the detail as I do. Until last Friday I worked for the police.'

His claim made an awkward, ugly sense. Like an unwelcome sexual advance, it embarrassed and silenced Abel.

'Follow me,' said Kidd.

He picked up the jars and stood, a jar in each hand, and pushed past Abel on his way out of the mess. Abel found him at the rail on the seaward side of the ship. The salt air was still, yet the flashing of the sea suggested motion. Abel could almost believe he was taking leave of the land.

Kidd had the jars in his arms, nursing them. 'We've been using this boat as part of an entrapment operation.'

We.

'You had me taking smack to Levin,' said Abel.

'The idea was to see where it went. Think of a squirt of dye injected into the system and allowed to circulate.'

'But Bluntcuff and Keys were after you.'

'Colouring my image. Consolidating my cover.' The sun was a circle of gloss on his high forehead. 'We've almost sealed the ports, the points of entry. In a couple of years' time, there'll be no more heroin entering New Zealand. Anyone wanting a taste will have to become a chemist.'

Kidd stood one of the jars on the deck. He began to unscrew the lid from the other. Abel watched the lid spin down toward the water. Then Kidd extended his arm over the rail and inverted the jar. When it had voided itself of its contents, Kidd let it fall.

'I thought of you as a radical malcontent. I knew Vietnam had taught you cynicism, but I didn't know how much.'

'I was never in Vietnam. I never saw the things I described.' Only this last admission seemed to cause him shame. He picked up the second jar. And began to loosen its lid, thoughtfully. 'I shouldn't have lied to you about Vietnam.'

'You're a sinister self-deluding mendacious scab.'

'But protective of the young.'

He emptied the second jar over the rail. The powder fell away in a gout, a flung white splash worth thousands of dollars.

Forty-eight

I left the ship relieved and empty-handed. I felt the exhilaration that follows a close shave, a reprieve. I had supped with the devil and may have stunk of sulphur, but I wasn't on my way to the burns ward.

Guy was in the bar in which I'd met Electra. 'How was your man?' he asked.

'He tipped my morphine over the side of a boat. Omar Kidd turned out to be a cop.'

'What did you say to get bail so quick?'

My narrative was informed by a sense of surprised escape. 'Do you think these events will follow me through life?'

'Bound to, I imagine. The stuff of apprehension and nightmare.' Guy winked that solemn, comforting wink of his.

We drank. Late that afternoon, I got on the train. Guy had had to give me the fare. I slept on the shady side of the antiquated carriage. The station at Rabbit Bay is remote from the village and the beach. I faced a long trudge into the sun.

It was a Tuesday in early December. From the mountains to the sea, the air was clear. Summer was beginning in earnest. On his way through the village Abel risked a look into the window of the pharmacy. Bedecked by green tinsel, crimson parcels disgorged Lenthèric and Jade East toiletries. Instamatic cameras and Kodak films tumbled from capsized Christmas boxes. Abel saw sunglasses with smoky amber lenses.

No haze clouds the air this afternoon. Abel continues his walk toward the beach, the end of Pa Road and Freddie West's house. He reaches the wide and shaggy macrocarpa under which Marika met Guy Ace.

I imagined an autopsy to be a peeling away of layers, the tweezered stretching of membranes. (A pricking of sacs. The penetration of moist atria.) Electra's drowning had followed a convulsion, but where would the evidence be hidden? The coroner released her body at last. On the 13th of December 1976, Conrad and I attended the Karori crematory. Lincoln was absent; Marika didn't show up. It was a hollow ceremony. Electra's coffin moved backward on a conveyor belt. Toy curtains closed on it. Only months later did the coroner speak. One shouldn't swim at night; the actions of Lincoln Dorne on the night of the tragic fatality had been exemplary.

Watchful, shy, dry-eyed, Electra's mother stood on the wet gravel. She was dressed in a dark suit. Her husband introduced Conrad. There in the small crowd outside the crematorium, Conrad looked presentable enough in his borrowed blazer. I had made him shave. Electra's bereaved mother pressed my brother's hand between her own two gloved ones. He was a piece of her daughter's life and she had trusted her daughter. Mrs Begg was a woman who seemed about to depart, to quit the company, albeit regrettably, and in spite of her very conspicuous beauty. I saw that any knowledge of her must be based on an understanding of her shyness. But here was Conrad and Conrad was real; Conrad was flesh and blood.

'My poor dear boy. So puzzled and lost. I want you to come to the house.'

And Conrad went, but that's another story.

His exhibition was five years taking place. When he had destroyed or reworked or given away most of his best pictures, he hung a dozen canvases, economical and timid, a trite compendium of good intentions. He regressed in his talent like Utrillo, producing what was of less and less interest. He married a woman as lazy and gay as himself. And bought himself the tools of household maintenance. He climbed makeshift scaffolds; he pulled nails and drilled, speaking from cavities in the ceiling. There appeared on the connubial mantelpiece the photograph I had given him, of himself as an infant in our mother's arms. And yet when his first child was born he told me, 'I can be sure of this. I know where this came from.' His daughter pursed her tiny lips; there were grains of sawdust in Conrad's hair. Marriage agreed with him. The muddle and soggy cereal and outings softened and stilled him. As his children grew they got into his paints and he ceased to care for what was whole and unmuddied, the tidy vectors of adult endeavour. He designed a new kind of napkin. Accept the claims I make; embrace what I tell you.

Abel reaches the house. He heads for the room in which he will find Marika, the bedroom he shares with her. It is not his fault that he moves quietly, that he was taught to carry himself through the world with a minimum of violence, avoiding concussion and collision, eschewing occasions of gracelessness and clatter, steering clear of the furniture and dodging potholes. His unconscious stealth is rewarded by a sight of the utmost straightforwardness. He has let himself in for it and here it is. It goes to his solar plexus via his neck; it thrills and nauseates; it challenges belief in reason and belief; it saddens.

They are naked. Marika is on the bed on her hands and knees. Lincoln is kneeling in front of her.

Not himself – but Lincoln. Not Conrad – but Lincoln.

Lincoln has his penis in his hand and is feeding it to Marika. Abel has asked for this, that her mouth be full of cock, that he should catch her eating.

There are two privacies, Abel's and theirs. Each is exposed to the other in this instant.

Marika is the one who looks up. Lincoln's taut erection is upwardly curved. It glistens because it is covered in saliva. But what can Marika's glance be said to express?

Abel withdraws to the kitchen. Perhaps he should leave the house. He picks up a cup from the bench. He tosses it into the air and bats it to the floor, hurting his knuckles. He picks up the tarnished toaster and crashes it down on the stove. He had thought of her as his bride.

The kitchen windows and living-room doors were open. From outdoors came the noise of cicadas. Abel fingered the toaster he had broken. He waited as if for the next event in a sequence.

When she had dressed, Marika showed herself. 'A situation developed,' she said.

'Your precious sexual needs.'

'It's no big deal. Relax.'

'As long as your precious needs are being met.'

'It's funny in a way.'

'I offered you something. I was giving you something of value. But now we know what you'll settle for instead.'

'These things happen. Forget it.'

'He's an attractive guy. You prefer him to me.'

'And you prefer him to me.'

'What's that supposed to mean?'

'Your friendships are more important to you than me.'

'Nothing's more important to me than you.'

The cicadas scraped. Abel was hot and thirsty. Lincoln passed on his way to the caravan. 'And you can get the fuck out,' Abel told him.

'I though you believed in tolerance or whatever.'

'Out.'

'I can't move the Citröen till I've fixed it.'

'You and your bloody wrecks.'

'Not wrecks.'

'The place is looking like a fucking slum.'

'Only from the back.'

'Stay. Go. I couldn't care bloody less.'

There would be other women, many very sweet. But we flash outwards from that first implosion, poisonous tides of light.

Tiny beads of rain, the stuff of mist

My life would continue in another place. I felt oafish and unattractive, ashamed of my own emotions. It worried me that I might never again know what a woman promised, just what her smile expressed.

Marika left the following Friday. An agency with which she was registered wanted to interview her.

Lincoln drove the three of us to the station. A mist and a misty rain were seeping down from the hills.

'Wish me luck,' she said.

I kissed her on the lips. I think I must have kissed her.

And when the train had gone, Lincoln said, 'I hope I haven't caused anything.'

Tiny beads of rain had settled on his jersey. That much I recall.